FINN

XAVIER'S HATCHLINGS BOOK 1

KATHI S. BARTON

This is a work of fiction. Names, characters, places, and incidents are products of the author's imagination or are used fictitiously and are not to be construed as real. Any resemblance to actual events, locations, organizations, or persons, living or dead, is entirely coincidental.

World Castle Publishing, LLC
Pensacola, Florida
Copyright © Kathi S. Barton 2020
Paperback ISBN: 9781951642761
eBook ISBN: 9781951642778
First Edition World Castle Publishing, LLC, June 8, 2020
http://www.worldcastlepublishing.com

Cover: Karen Fuller
Editor: Maxine Bringenberg

Prologue

Long ago, at a time when all creatures roamed the earth as only their true selves, working with and helping humans in whatever way they could. Where magic was celebrated, and dragons darkened the skies every day. It was then man discovered there was magic in the dragons, and hunted them almost to extinction.

"I'm afraid there is no hope for us." No one made a sound as their leader continued. "Since the humans found out about us and what we can do for them dead, we have been doomed. I'm so terribly sorry."

Coop looked around the cave. There were so few of them now he could easily count them. When he had been younger, thousands of years ago, there would not have been enough space for all of them to share this cave. Now they were down to having a quarter of them left, because so many, his own wife included, had been murdered so needlessly. Coop was saddened by it all.

Turning to leave the large cave, he was stopped by his brother, Xavier.

"The boys, they are well?" He nodded and smiled. Coop felt it all the way to his heart, a place that had been dead for so long, it seemed. "You have the spell? You are going to use it on them? I so wish I had thought of this before my own family was taken from me, Coop. You are a brave man and a good father."

"Thank you. And I shall use it tonight. It is the only way to save them." Xavier nodded, his own heart heavy with the losses they had suffered. "You know I would have shared should I have had it sooner. I am so sorry, Brother. All of my heart, it's sorry for you."

"I know that. I do. But they are all gone now—my other half, my children. Killed for things not fair to our kind." Coop knew all too well. "Aria was a good woman, Coop. A good woman and mother to your sons. She will be missed forever."

"Aye, in my heart and those of my sons." Xavier stood there for several seconds, and Coop told him he must go. "They're awaiting word on what is to happen with us all."

"One more thing, if you please. It will not take but a second. I have left them all I have. It is where you keep them hidden away, the boys. Deep within the cave, it's all there." Coop asked him what he meant. "I cannot go on, Brother. I cannot. There is too much grief in my heart for me to live. I have left my things for them there. They might survive this, with the magic you have to give them. And if so, they'll need more than you have to help them."

"Xavier, please, you mustn't do this. They'll miss you as much as I." Xavier nodded and said it had begun. "You can come and stay with them. You'll live with them in the caves."

"Nay. I cannot. I must go. Just tell them I love them, with all of my heart." There would be no stopping him once his heart was made up. Coop knew this, but it made his heart ache no less for it. "Goodbye, my brother. Take care you are not caught by the humans."

Coop made his way back to his hidden cave and sat before the fire. The boys, he knew, were resting, their bodies getting stronger daily with their age. Soon they would be as big as him, dragons of worth and size. When his eldest son came to him, his eyes full of fear, Coop knew it was well past time for him to do what he had been practicing. The magic would keep them safe.

Gathering his sons, six of them of varying shades of blues and greens, he asked them to have a seat, that he had a story to tell them. It was not a story, not truly, but a tale that would hopefully keep them safe.

"A witch told me once of a great magic, only a few can do. It takes a loving heart and a strong dragon to make it work. I have asked her, and she has told me how to make it so. This magic, it will keep you all safe from the humans." They nodded, each of them knowing it was a human blade that had taken the life of their dear mother. "I will perform this upon you, each of you at the same time, and give you some magic you will use when you need it. This magic, strong and powerful, will let you roam with the humans, and they'll not know your true self is just below your flesh."

"You mean we'll be humans as well?" He nodded, then shook his head at Cooper, his oldest. "I don't understand, Father. Will you explain?"

"Yes. The magic I will give you will let you change into your true self when you are alone. But when you are out in the world, you will need to be a human. A man." Cooper looked at his brothers, then back at him as he continued. "With this magic, I will also give you a gift. Something you will need to keep yourself safe should they find out. A stronger armor than any other dragon before you, as well as the same immortality you have now, as man or dragon."

Hudson stared at him for long moments. He was the thinker, and if he could think of a reason for this not to work, he would voice it loudly. He was much like his mother in that. She would be the first to say when she did or did not like something. And the first to say the plan was perfect. He only hoped she would have approved of this.

"I think you are very smart, Father, to try and keep us safe. But I can only think this will not work on you. Or is that your plan?" The boy was much too smart, Coop thought. "If you change us, who will change you?"

"There will be no one to change me, son. I will.... It is my wish to join your mother in this earth." He watched them, seeing if they understood the love he had lost when she was murdered. "Giving you this magic, it will be something I can tell her I've done for her sons. You know as well as I, she loved you more than anything on this earth, including herself."

"She died saving us." Coop nodded at Lincoln. "I'm not happy you're going to die, Father, but I understand wanting to be with Mother. I miss her more every day."

"As do I." He looked at his sons, all of them growing into dragons of worth. "I must have an agreement from you all. Even if one of you does not want this, then it will not work. I would say you should think on this hard. For once I have given this to you, there will be no going back."

"I wish to have it." He had known Cooper would be the first. Not that he did not love his father, but Cooper would see things in a way most would not. To not do this would mean certain death for them all. Dragons were too valuable dead not to be hunted for all time. "I will do whatever it takes to make sure you are proud of me, as well."

"I am already, Cooper. Forever."

The others nodded too. They were ready for this as much as he was dreading it. Because once he started the process to change his sons into men, he would begin to die. It would take all he was to change them.

Standing up, spreading his wings out behind him, Coop told them about the things their uncle had left them. They knew where the family jewels were, the things their mother had left them as well. Once they were standing, their bodies strong and healthy, he felt his heart swell and break for what he was about to do.

"I, Cooper Manning, of the Manning Dragons of the earth, give to my sons, Cooper, Hudson, Lincoln, Lucas, Tristan, and Xavier, all that I am. Each of you will take a part of the earth with you when you are converted. The part of you that is unique in all ways will be strengthened and enhanced. You will be immortal, forever, and those you take to your heart will be as well." His sons bowed before him when he told them to. He said the words over them that would change them to men. Coop could feel his body shutting down, his heart beating a little more slowly. But he had one more thing he wished to bless them with, and held himself upright to give it from his own dying heart. "One day, true love will come to you. And you will have more than you have ever known. It will fill you in ways you cannot even imagine. Love will be yours for all time. For only then will you become a true dragon, a Manning Dragon."

~~~

Cooper sat with his brothers while their father lay dying. Coop's heart was weak from what he had done, and it was tearing Cooper apart. Father was weak, yes, but he continued to tell them tales of their mother, of their adventures when they were only small dragons. They were going to be alone soon; their father was so close to joining their mother; it hurt Cooper in ways he had not expected.

"What shall we do with his body?" Cooper looked at Tristan and asked him what he meant. "He will not be able to lie here. If the humans were to find him, they would surely cut him up into pieces. I do not want that for him. We were never able to bury Mother in the proper way after what they did to her."

"We could burn his body." Cooper wondered how it would work when Hudson continued. "His scales will be worthless to them should they come upon his body. The magic he held within him also will be useless to them. He will be nothing more than a carcass. They'll leave him alone."

Burn his body — it was something to think about. But he did not want to, not while he was still breathing, his body still alive. When he laid his head upon his father's chest, hearing his heart beating slower and slower, Cooper wondered what his father would think if he knew the magic he had given them had not worked. They were all still dragons.

"He gave his life to keep us safe. But it did not work." No one said anything to him as they each watched their father.

"Dragons such as us, we'll be hunted and killed by the humans. There is nothing we can do but wait for them."

"We will survive if we stay here." Cooper told Xavier they would have to leave here eventually. "To feed and to fly, yes. But perhaps we could do it only at night. To keep to the skies and not let them see us."

"They know we are about and will have spies out looking for our lairs. We will have to kill any man should he come for us, and still, we will not be safe. We are, after all, dragons who have a great deal of magic."

Coop stopped breathing. Cooper did not hear his father's heart and knew it was at an end. He was quiet for a bit longer, waiting, hoping for just one more beat, one more sound that would mean he was still alive. But there was nothing. Their father was dead.

Sitting up, Cooper told them their father had passed from this world into the next. None of them had ever seen a dragon die before. Their mother had been dead when they found her. Each dragon they had come upon when they were out had been dead long before they found them, their bodies stripped of every part, so they resembled more a pile of bones than a dragon.

Their scales were used by the humans for roofs for their homes and for shields. The very meat of them was roasted and stored away so it could be used for medicines and potions. Hearts were cut up and dried, then ground into a powder to use for other things the humans would use to keep them from sickness, as well as magic to have a grand garden and trees heavy with fruit. The only part that would be left was the bones, and sometimes even those were carried off and used for something. Cooper hated all humans.

"We will do as suggested by Hudson. It is the only assured way we can—"

Before he could finish, he felt the stirring of the earth. It shook so hard it knocked each of them off their feet. As they lay there, terrified someone was coming for them, their father appeared before them.

His body was still aground, but instead of dark in death, he was brilliant in light. Faeries, thousands upon thousands of faeries, seemed to be covering him. Before Cooper could tell them to stop, to leave him alone, Father spoke.

"I love you, my sons." Each of them nodded, fear almost something Cooper could touch. "I will now and forever join my true love, your mother. I must warn you, when you find your other halves, and you will, you will have to be careful of the slayers. They will know what you have found by the magic you both will share. My sons, you will leave this place and take your place among men. Becoming someone I will be proud of."

"Father, the magic didn't work. We're still dragons." Cooper felt shameful to say a thing to his father. To tell him his sacrifice had not worked. "We will be hunted and killed."

"Nay, you only need to think of being your other half. Becoming a man is simple. The same when you wish to be your true self." Cooper was not sure what that meant, but his father continued before he could ask. "Go now, before the men come. The magic to hide me will draw them here. Be safe, my sons, and know I love you more than I do any other creature on this earth."

Cooper stood then, the faeries still working, taking the body of his father apart. But as he watched, he could see they were not doing anything but preserving his body. Faerie ropes encircled him, strings of magic wrapping around him like a cocoon, making him invisible to all. As Cooper stood there, his brothers beside him, he knew, like him, they mourned the loss of yet another parent.

"You are the eldest." He nodded to the faerie when she asked. "We have a gift for you. For all of you, but you will receive the most. Your father was a great man, your mother, a queen among her people. We wish to bestow upon you all your father had."

"My brothers, they will need it as well. I should like to share." She smiled at him and bowed. "What have you done with his body?"

"He is being prepared to be moved. We will make a grand garden upon him. Flowers will be there for all to see, but only a few will know a dragon is there with his other half, his love." He nodded. It was as it should be. "You will take this gift? You will share, but as I said, you will get more than the others."

"I don't care. Please, just do what you must so we can hide." She nodded again and touched her fingers, tiny ones, to his forehead. Then she did the same to the others before coming back to him. "It is done? You have shared it with us?"

"I have, Lord Cooper. But you must leave here now. There are humans coming. The magic we used to do this thing has given them cause to come here." He nodded and looked at the ground where their father had been. "He is safe. Just as your mother is now. Go, before they find you here and murder you as well."

He thanked her for her help and left. The exit from this part of the cave was hidden so well only they knew about it. As they made their way into the night, he thought of the human inside of him, and the pain of it took his breath away. In seconds he was down on his knees. Whatever was happening, he was surely going to die.

"You're a man." He looked up at his brothers as they began to transfer to their human versions. "We'll be safe now, all of us. We'll be humans for them until we can find a safe place where we can be ourselves."

"I don't think that's ever going to happen." Hudson nodded and held his head tightly as he did so. "We will need to train ourselves in their ways. Become what they are. But never monsters."

"No, never." They made their way to a building; any would do for now. Hudson, like Cooper, was staggering a little, but they were getting stronger as they moved. He turned to look at him as they were settling in the empty shell of a house. "We will need to buy things, houses and such."

"Yes. But tomorrow. I am too tired to think beyond how much we have lost." Hudson and the others agreed. "When the humans are gone from our cave, we'll go and find what Father was telling us about earlier, the wealth that will keep us safe."

"I only hope there is a great deal of it. I don't know how to work." Cooper told Xavier, the youngest brother, they would soon learn. "I hope so. I hope so."

He did, as well. It was going to be hard enough for them to learn to eat and dress like humans, much less get around. Cooper hoped this worked, for he was as afraid as he had ever been in his life.

~~~

After a time, thousands of years, each of the dragons,

turned into men, forged their way into a world so different than the one they had been born to it seemed a different planet. But survive they did.

Having their mates come to them, children born to all of them gave them hope. A small and fragile thing after such hardships they had been born to. Cooper became, as his father had been before him, the king of dragons—his mate, Carson, their queen. It had been and still was a time for celebration. To this day, they commemorated often and hard at each new birth of the dragons turned men and women.

The others, his brothers, prospered too, finding their other halves, making their magic stronger for having their love. They worked hard in keeping everyone safe and well fed, humans or other dragons. No one, not anyone in need, was ever turned away from their help. The Manning Dragons, true to their father and mother, became the most powerful dragons ever born.

Of the six sons, Xavier's sons, four hatchlings and two humans, moved far away to be the next generation of Manning Dragons who would open their hearts and doors for all creatures. Even the sons of his heart, the two human born men, carried a powerful magic. They used it, with their brothers, to help as many people as possible, humans and dragons alike, to live in the ever changing world. To help them not only succeed but to, perhaps, help someone else when they needed it. These boys, now men, have stories to tell.

Chapter 1

Finn wasn't thrilled about the way things were piling up on his desk. Just yesterday, he'd asked his faerie, Bell, to see if she could find a way for him to be able to see the top of his desk. Her *help* was to push it all to the trash can. Even after she filled it, Bell continued to toss things to the floor. She could be spiteful when the mood struck her.

"How is that even remotely helpful?" She asked him if there was anything else piled on his desk. "No, there isn't. However, now it's on the floor, and still in a state of messiness. I wanted to see if you could help me organize it, not just find the top of my desk for me."

"Organize it? I can." With the snap of her fingers, not only was everything back on his desk, but also in neat piles. Each pile, she told him, was for one of the many companies he was working with. "You should take better care of your things, your lordship. Your mother would be so very disappointed in you."

"I'm sure she would be. If she were here." He looked

around to make sure she was not nearby watching him. Just in case. "I love her to pieces, but I don't think there is another person in the world who can be as organized and neat as my mom is. Dad is even better organized since they got together, I'm to understand."

"He is." Bell was today helping him look through the paperwork one pile at a time. "You need yourself someone to come in here and sort this for you. Not just to make piles, but to see what you need to work on. It's too much, and you will not work here because it's too much."

"I know. But I don't even know where to begin to hire someone." He looked over the paperwork for the new building he'd commissioned to go in months ago. "I think I need to make myself a list of things that should have been finished by now and go inspect them. I don't think some of these projects, even from months ago, have even been started."

"They have not." She looked over his shoulder at the folder he was currently holding onto. "Aye, Master. I would think it should have been completed many weeks ago. I know for a fact we would have had it completed had you allowed us to take the job over."

"I've not even mentioned we're dragons living here. Can you imagine their faces when they see a building go up overnight, let alone be ready for occupants? They'd think themselves nuts." Finn laughed a little. "I guess it would be easier to explain who and what we are if something like that were to happen."

He put the paper down and laid his head down on his desk. Even for the number of hours they'd been working, Finn had barely put a dent into what he had left to go over. Reaching out to his aunt, he asked Carson if she could find him someone who would be willing to work for him. It was all he could think to do and have someone he could trust in the office.

I can do that. I'm glad you finally got your head out of your ass and figured out you can't do it all on your own. Bell has been complaining about the mess in there for weeks now. How about those two projects I sent you? Have you had any luck finding out if the buildings have been started or not? He told her that was his next project, to go around checking on projects. *Could you please send Bell to check on them? The company that is supposed to be doing the work is saying they're over budget and time. I think he's full of shit, but that could just be me.*

Finn told Bell what he needed her to do for Carson. When she left him, he looked around his office again. Christ, it really was a huge mess. He should have, as Carson said, gotten his head out of his ass long ago.

Okay, I have three names I'm going to send you through email. It will also have their stats and pictures. I know you need computer help too. Not that you can't run one, but it will free you up for all the other projects going on for the Manning Foundation. She told him the names, and Finn pulled the email up when his computer dinged, telling him he had a message. *I'll send them in order on the list. They've all been bonded. One of them is a dragon, but I don't think the two of you will get along very well.*

Why is that? She told him. *Okay, then don't send her. I don't need someone who will be bitching at me about things around my house that are no concern of hers. While I have you, I was also wondering how I would go about finding someone to come here and cook for me. It's not really a big deal, but I think I'll get fewer stares when I order food if I don't have to explain why I'm having three meals instead of just the one humans eat.*

I can understand. I'll find someone to come around for cooking as well. How are the others doing, Finn? I know you guys decided staying together as a family would make it easier for you to adjust, but I do worry about George and Milo. They have a great deal less magic than the rest of you, and I don't want them to think they're not going to be able to do this job. He told her what he'd figured out. *Oh, so they're doing better than you guys are. It shouldn't surprise me, but it really does. I'm assuming by you telling me they're getting out more, you mean they're dating more than the rest of you.*

Yes. That about sums it up. Don't get me wrong — every woman who sees where we live automatically assumes we're prime meat. Big house, single man. Scary. I mean, I was picking up something at the hardware store the other day and had to leave without buying anything. Aunt Carson, I had women — with their men — following me around trying to look like they weren't following me around. Laughing with him, Carson asked him if they should have gone with a smaller house to start with. *No. I love the houses you guys picked out for us. All of them are perfect. Mine couldn't have been better if I had told you what I wanted. And the pool is perfect for cooling me down.*

I had to search for a while to find you a home with a pool. I knew, as a red dragon, you'd need it worse than the others.

He ran hot, molten hot, all the time. And when the weather was humid and above eighty, he could literally sweat buckets. Lucky for him, he was able to control it better than he had been when he was younger. And the pool took so much pressure off him when he had to stay as a human for more than a day or two.

When they made arrangements for her to start sending him people who could potentially work for him, he nearly closed the connection. Then Bell returned, looking like she'd been hit a couple of times. Finn could feel his dragon getting the better of them.

"They did not care for me looking around the building, Master. It was as if they were prepared for someone to come and see how it was progressing." He asked her what had happened. "Those men will not try and capture me in a net again. I made them hurt badly. But the building isn't finished. There isn't even any equipment there to indicate anyone has wanted to start on it for Lady Carson."

He relayed the information to his aunt, and she wasn't the least bit surprised. After she told him she'd be there in a couple of days, he decided he wanted to give this a go on his own. It was what they'd been sent there for, to make sure the money they were lending out went to what it was supposed to, and to people who were actually in need of the money. So far, all he'd been able to do was chase down people, which was why he was so far behind.

I think I'd like to – I'll take care of this. She didn't ask him if he was sure. Finn was both surprised and terrified by that thought. *You send me what you have on the person I'm to talk with, and I'll go and see what is going on.*

Don't go alone. Laughing, Finn asked her if she thought he was nuts. When she laughed as well, he felt better. *I know you can handle whatever comes your way, Finn. I have no doubt you can make sure this job gets done. But it sounds like this person is spoiling for a fight, and I don't want you to lose your shit over this.*

I'll be extra careful. I'll take George with me. He's calming. His brother was the one person who could bring him back from nearly losing his shit, as Aunt Carson had said. *We'll figure out which of the men hurt Bell, too. Once this is cleaned up, I'm going to need to start taking a bigger role in this project. I've been here for six months, and all I've managed to do is drown myself in paperwork.*

As I said before, it's about time. Nodding though he knew she couldn't see him, he felt better already. *I'll send what I have to you in an email. I'll also send you hard copies. I think there might be a driver's license picture in with the file as well. His name is Jack Bash.*

She told him everything would be in the file, but it was nice to have his notes too. When his computer dinged once again, he pulled it up to look at it, just to make sure he didn't have any questions for her.

Finn was still going over things when George joined him a little while later. Not only did he have a lot more notes to arm himself with, but he also had a little more background on the person he was seeing—or going to try and see. Finn told George what they were doing.

"Thank goodness." They both laughed. "I'm going out of my mind just sitting around doing shit. It's like we took all this time to find a place that would be central to Manning Foundation, moved here, and now we're doing nothing but sitting on our collective asses. I'm ready for something to do."

"I was thinking of not making an appointment to see this person and just showing up unannounced. What do you think?" George told him it was great, then he couldn't hide from them when the time came. "He or his men tried to hurt Bell too. I need to make sure he understands I won't put up with that sort of treatment."

"I don't want to cause trouble either. But this is getting out of hand. Not with this situation, but the one I'm working on. I have several bids to revamp the grade school gym. So far, I can't find any of the bidders who put in a bid. The only person I have been able to talk to is one of their secretaries, who tells me he's out of town on a business trip. I ask you, what sort of business trip takes six months?" Finn told him the avoidance kind. "Yes, I think so too. He's not going to get anything on my end until I can verify a couple of things. For instance, why is it costing nearly a million dollars to have two new basketball nets replaced on the backboards that are already there and, by all accounts, in perfect shape? I can't even get into this school to see what the problem is on my own. I was honestly trying not to ask someone to get me in, so I'd not feel like I'm falling down on the job."

"I asked Aunt Carson for help. You know what she told me? 'Thank goodness you got around to getting your head out of your ass.' I was much nicer, just so you know." They were both laughing when Finn spoke again. "If you don't ask her for help, I will. And you know that won't go over well for her. She's in a good mood. Well, as good a mood as you can expect out of her."

"I love her, but there are times when I don't want to tell her anything." They loaded up in his SUV. "How do you like this thing? I know you got a truck as well when we were vehicle shopping, but I've only seen you driving around in this. It seems small to me."

"Nah. I love it. And since its usually just me or one other person, I keep the seat lying down. It's roomy enough for just running around town." A flash of light reminded him he'd not asked Bell to come with them. He told her he was sorry. "I didn't think to ask you, Bell, because I thought you'd had enough of them already. I'm sorry."

"I cannot protect you if you do not tell me where you are going." He told her it was why he had George. "George is a good choice to keep you calm. I will help you kill them if they need it."

He wasn't sure if she was joking or not, so didn't say anything. As soon as he pulled into the parking lot of the building that was supposed to be worked on, he was glad for all the help he could get. Finn asked his brothers if any of them were close to his location. All four of them told him they were on their way to him now.

<center>~~~</center>

It was everything George could do not to laugh. It really was funny, but no one else standing in the parking lot seemed to think it was nearly as amusing as he did. Turning his back on Finn when he snorted with laughter again, he saw his brother Hadley laughing as hard as he was. Or at least trying not to laugh like he was.

"Are we at an agreement now?" The six men who had been standing around at the building site were battered and bruised. None of the brothers had a scratch on them. "When I or one of my representatives come here to check on the progress, at any time, you will have a crew working here, and they'll be progressing toward some sort of ending. This is what we agreed upon when the money was lent to you. Correct?"

"Yes, sir. We'll be here working. All of us. We'll be working hard in finishing up this building." The man speaking, the first one who had challenged Finn, was now nearly bowing to his brother and ready to agree to anything he wanted, George thought. "I'm going to take my entire crew off other projects to get this one here finished up. Just like I should have done in the first place."

"You should have had this entire building done by now. I cannot believe in six months you've not even put the first nail in the first piece of wood." The man, he didn't know his name, said it was entirely his fault. "I'm certainly not going to take the blame for this. You have a crew here in the morning or so help me, I will hunt you down, and what I showed you today will be nothing to what I will do to you in the morning."

He and Finn had gotten out of the car, both of them laughing about something Bell had told them about the man in the yellow shirt. It was she who had pointed out he was in the man in charge of the operation. On their way to confront the man, Finn simply bent at the waist and picked up a long piece of iron. It had to be heavy. The way his muscles had bulged out had made George think it might have been a little heavier than even Finn had thought it would be.

The man in the yellow shirt spoke first. "Well, well, well. If it isn't the Manning Foundation. I heard you guys were around and about. I was just talking to the one in charge there, telling her we're over budget and she's to send me some money. Or so I thought." The others laughed when he did. "I'm not sure how I can use a couple of pretty boys, but you come on and let me see what you can do and we'll—"

The iron in Finn's hands started to get hot. It might not have been noticeable at first, not while yellow shirt was talking, but as soon as it started to melt into a large puddle at his feet, Finn bent it in half and leaned on it.

"How the fuck did you do that?"

If the man hadn't been so focused on the red hot iron, he might well have noticed Finn was getting hot as well. His face was darkening, and his hands had small flames on them. When he put the piece of iron down on the ground, all he did was take a single small step towards yellow shirt.

Finn didn't show off. He didn't even like being hot when he was angry. But today he seemed to be having way too much fun for even George to tell him to back off. Finn touched his hand to the obviously new truck in the parking lot, and all of them watched as his hand went through the hood of the truck and deep into the engine compartment. When he came out with a handful of flaming parts, he blew on them, igniting the parts that weren't on fire already, and tossed them at the men.

George would laugh every time he thought of them trying to get away from the fire. There wasn't much to it after it left Finn's hand — just a few embers of whatever the part was. The men looked like it was a ball of flames set to turn them into ash. The rest of the family showed up and just leaned against their cars and waited.

The workers were falling all over themselves, knocking each other down, which accounted for their being battered and bruised — the Mannings never touched them. They were screaming like little girls when one of the others pushed them out of the way. It didn't even matter if they were pushed toward the now extinct fire — they were terrified, it seemed, that the sucker was going to start up again and take them out.

"Who thinks they're in charge here?" The entire group of them pointed at the man in yellow. Finn took a step toward the man and smiled at him. It wasn't friendly at all, George thought. "You want me to have to hunt you down? Show you what I did to this truck? Or are you going to get your fucking asses in gear and finish this building? I'm not a man who likes to repeat himself. Ever. If I have to come back here and see how my family's money is being used, then there will have to be an entirely new crew hired, because I will not tell you a second time you're to get your shit together and fucking finish this work. Do I make myself entirely clear?"

"Yes, sir. Yes, sir, I'm very clear on what has to be done here." The man looked like he was going to lose his head, he was bobbing it up and down so quickly. "I didn't know you were going to come here, or I would have had them start on it today."

"You piece of shit, you should have had this done by now. Christ, do you have any idea how many offers we've had to come here and do the job correctly? More than I like to hear about. You'll start on this tomorrow, bright and early, or I swear to you on my mother's heart I will not be happy." The man was tossing out assignments even as Finn continued. "If I or any of my brothers come by here at any time during usual business hours and there isn't a crew working on this, you won't have to worry about paying back the money the foundation already paid you. I'm going to roast you fucking alive. Understand?"

Finn then turned to the rest of them, and it was Dover who gave him the thumbs up. George could tell they were all impressed with Finn, but he could also tell Finn wasn't all that happy with himself. It wasn't like him to make a scene about something. The man rarely lost his temper either. It was much too dangerous for it to happen.

George caught the car keys when they were tossed at him. He wondered if Finn was going to be able to get into the car, what with him still being hot. But once he was in the seat and buckled, the rest of them got into their cars as well. George didn't ask any of them but pulled into the first place to eat he came upon. It just happened to be a steak house.

No one spoke to anyone as they were seated and given menus. Finn ordered a large glass of water, as did the rest of them. They'd not drink theirs but would hand it to Finn to help him cool off. The more he looked at Finn, the more he realized he wasn't going to need it. He looked as well as he had before they'd left the house.

"May I ask you a question?" He nodded at Milo when he spoke to Finn. "Why did you call us? I mean, it looked to me like you had things well under control. I was surprised, I will tell you, but I think you did just what needed to be done. I think—and this is just me—but I think I'm going to stop being such a pussy and take charge as you did today."

"I hated that." Milo told Finn he was glad he hated it. "I know. I don't want to have to show that side of me ever again. I know I will have to going forward, but it'll be less and less as they understand we're here to do a job the same as they are. However, I do agree with you, Milo. I think we do need to show enough of ourselves to make these people we're trying to help see that we're not pushovers."

"I don't think they'll think of you as a pushover again." Hadley laughed when he spoke. "Did you noticed Kimble pissed himself?" George asked who that was. "The guy in the yellow shirt. I swear to Christ, when you tossed those wires at them, I nearly pissed myself. Laughing hard had never felt so good before."

When the water was brought to them, Finn said he was fine, he didn't need theirs. George asked him about that, why he'd been so quick to cool down. His answer surprised him—

surprised them all, George thought.

"I wasn't ever angry. I was upset, yes, but never angry. I was walking up there and told myself I was going to walk away angry. However, in picking up the iron, which I was going to toss in the dumpster as we walked by it, I thought, I can end this shit right now." Finn laughed a little more. "You won't believe how easy it was to control the fire too. I've never had much control over myself. Ever. It was as if I let a little out there to show them I wasn't fucking around. Then after a little bit of steam was let off, I had unbelievable control. I think I could have shot my flames at something and hit it. I'm thinking this is exactly what Dad was trying to tell me when he said I needed to focus not on what I could do if it got away from me, but what I could do if I could control it."

By the time their orders were taken, word must have gotten around about what had happened at the job site. The waitress asked them if they'd really set fire to Kimble's truck, and Finn told her he had a job to do, and Kimble wasn't doing it. Afterwards, several people came by to ask them if any of them could fire Kimble up to do the jobs he'd been paid for by them. Things people had been waiting on longer than the Mannings had on this particular job.

George realized as they were being brought their salads that not one of the people had asked them what they were, or how Finn had been able to do what he'd done. They were just glad, it seemed, that someone had stood up to a bully, and come out on top.

The stories they were being told about Kimble and his men were much of the same thing—jobs being paid for up front and never finished. It was also pointed out to them that no one even bid against Kimble on jobs anymore because they'd lose out on things.

"What sort of things?" The man, he thought his name was Rider, said he'd lost his garage when something was tossed into it. Another man and his wife said the tires on their car had been slashed. Theo was shaking his head when he continued speaking. "We don't condone their sort of work ethics. I want you to know that right now. I tell you what, if you can have everyone bring me a list of the things that aren't finished, I'll make sure they are. We'll even bring in a crew of our own men to do it."

Before they left the restaurant, they had five names of people who had been dealt a shitty hand by Kimble. Theo was going to put together the list when he got as many names as he could and then would take care of them. Dover told Finn he'd work on getting another crew lined up, and George suggested he call Carson and see if the pack there wanted to work with the one here.

"What a good idea. I know our old pack was working construction. If they could come here and get these guys trained if they need it, that'll make things so much easier for the next contract." Dover looked at him. "Thanks, George. I have to say, we might have hit on something here. We've been working at separate jobs here while trying to get things moving. Maybe we need to pool our knowledge and ideas and work as a unit. I know I've gotten more done since we sat here than I have in a while. What do you think, brothers? We're a team or a failure in this?"

Team, of course. Tomorrow morning George was going to have a video meeting with Carson. Then they were going to work together from now on. George thought this was the only way they were going to make this work. To work as a team while getting the foundation set up to help people who really needed it.

Chapter 2

It had taken him most of the day to get things organized the way his new secretary had told him to figure out. Finn had balked at first, thinking it should have been her job, but April had a good point. How would he find things if she were to have a day off if he didn't know the system? So he'd figured out what worked best for him, and tomorrow he'd show her what he'd figured out. It was a great deal more work than he'd thought it would have been.

"Master?" He looked at Bell, not even trying to get her to stop calling him master anymore. "I have some information on the other buildings Lady Carson asked us to have a look at. The men from the pack are there working today. Not only that, they have done quite a bit more than I thought they should have for such a job."

"Good. I'm glad we were able to talk to the pack leader last night. He did tell us his men would take over the jobs we needed and do a good job of it." Bell told him it was very fortuitous they also had a pack that needed money. "I don't know if I'd call it fortuitous or not, but it will help both of us that they need work. I think we're going to be able to do a lot of things for the pack, and in return, they'll be a great help to us as well."

Peter Duncan had a medium sized pack. However, it was almost all older people. Peter had told him there were only three couples still able to breed, and with that, he thought in a couple of years he'd have to find places for the people that were left.

"There aren't any jobs out there the men in my pack can do." Finn had thought they'd not be able to make it work between the two groups, but Peter brightened up for a second. "Unless you know someone who can hire some older men that have been working with their hands for most of their lives. Most of the pack was in construction. There isn't much of that going on around here."

"Great." Peter just stared at him. "This is exactly what we need. Construction and finishers. I have three buildings that need some work done on them. I had thought we'd have to start over on the lot of them, but one of my uncles came to look at the buildings and told me not only were they sound, but they should last for a great many more years. The pay is very good, and there are benefit packages to those who would like to have them. Like retirement and incentives they can participate in. Insurance is included as well."

"Are you seriously offering my pack jobs? And willing to pay them?" Finn had told him he was, as a matter of fact. "You have no idea.... When I heard a group of dragons had moved here, I had a feeling it was to take my pack from me. I have no idea why it entered my head, but the more I thought about it, the more it made sense. I mean, I've heard of larger groups, not necessarily dragons, coming in and taking over smaller packs of any shifter, and using them as farmhands and whatever else they needed."

"We'd never do anything of the kind. My family, we've been around for some time now, and we want to make things better for the surrounding areas. Hire locals when we can. Not only improve the land around us but bring in jobs. More than we can provide. My dad and uncles have a great setup with the pack near them." Peter asked why they'd come here. "To diversify. My brothers and I are the first to leave the family in order to see if there are more of our kind out there who need help to, as I said, improve the area they're in. To me, it's a win-win situation for all of us."

That had been last night. So the fact the men were working out at the first job site already showed him how much what Peter had said was true. The pack needed jobs — if not for the money, which they did need, then for the work. Being idle, his dad had told him, could lead to all kinds of trouble for anyone.

Standing up and stretching, Finn made his way to the kitchen. The new cook, Peter's mother, Mildred, was standing at the stove speaking to someone. It wasn't until he came all the way into the room that he noticed it was a faerie. Finn smiled when they both looked at him, and then Mildred asked him to have a seat, she needed to speak with him.

Sitting down, he saw a plate of sugar cubes on a small plate, as well as flower petals. He looked at the faerie when he didn't touch the treat. Something wasn't right here. Finn asked Mildred if she was getting along all right. He watched Sheppard, the new faerie to the house, as he sat there looking dejected.

"I'm not sure, sir. I've never worked with a little person before. But this one said he can help me in any way I wish. I'm not sure what that means, as he is having a bit of trouble making me understand. It's not his fault. I just don't understand, if he can do all he says he can, why you might need me around." The faerie introduced himself as Sheppard to Mildred. "I'm not trying to make any trouble here."

"Nay. You're not. Working with a faerie is something that can be difficult to a new person. Yes, he can cook for me and the rest of the family, but it's not his specialty." Finn was hoping she'd get it without him having to insult poor Sheppard. Again. "You see, his name is Sheppard for a reason. He's a herder of sheep and other animals. Not that he can do the job of a dog, but he does remind the animals when they need it to keep with the rest of their herd."

Mildred nodded, but he could tell she still didn't understand Sheppard was the worst cook he'd ever had in a kitchen. The grilled cheese he'd made for Finn just the other day had been covered in honey, and cookies were in the middle along with the cheese. Finn and his brother Milo had gagged several times, hurting the little man's feelings terribly.

He looked at Mildred when she laughed just a little.

"Oh. He's not—Sheppard here isn't used to cooking for such large men. Yes, I can see where that would be a problem with dragons in the home." She winked at him. "Oh Sheppard, I think the two of us will get along fabulously. Yes. With your talent of getting me fresh herbs and vegetables year round, I think the two of us will keep these men full all the time."

When she put out her hand for him, Finn was worried

Sheppard wasn't going to take it. But he touched his hand to her finger and smiled. Finn was so happy with the outcome he wanted to get up and jump for joy. For the first time in days, he'd been able to solve a problem.

Not really, but it was beginning to feel something akin to it. He'd been a failure, in his own eyes, over this move. Things weren't moving as quickly as he'd hoped they would. His fear was he'd disappoint his family, especially his parents.

After having some lunch of roast beef subs and French fries, he was ready to tackle the next thing on his list. It wasn't as daunting as the filing cabinet had been, but it was just as time consuming. When he went to get into his car, his brother Theo was there smiling a huge smile.

"What have you been up to?" Theo told him he was so glad he'd asked. He had good news. "Well, share it, Brother. I'm needing some great news about now."

"The three buildings that were going to be taken down near the orchard are now ours. I know we were going to move slowly, but I have an idea to expand the orchard and then have the faeries working on it. It's far enough off the beaten path no one will notice it's producing so quickly, and the stall in the front of it is large enough I think we could sell off some of the other products they've been working on." Finn asked him what products. "Oh, I forgot. When we were trying our best to make this work separately, I started a garden. It's a lot larger than I thought when I first had the idea. You know how faeries can be when they're excited. Anyway, I have corn and tomatoes, plus some potatoes that have been just waiting for me to find a place to put them. I don't want to sell them for money, but Holly told me if I were to give them away, the people would fear there was something wrong with it. Or, and this one surprised me, they'd think we were thinking they couldn't afford it, and it would hurt their feelings. I don't want to start off on a bad note."

They rode over to the place Theo was talking about. The buildings were in bad repair, but he'd learned a couple of things from when his dad had been here testing the wellness of a building. It really wasn't the wellness, he supposed, but something more like its strength. The first one he touched was sad and ready to be torn down. He told Theo what he'd felt.

"I can't do that." Finn told him it was the first time he'd done it since they'd been here. "Tell me what the other two are doing, and we'll work from there. I want to get started on the stall as soon as possible. The faeries are inundating me with foodstuff."

The second building had a strong foundation, but the roof needed to be replaced as well as the electrical components. The electrical was something he could do easily, and the roof would be repaired by the faeries. Almost as if he had called for them, they were there in force to fix not just the roof, but the interior as well. While they worked on that with Theo, he went to the third building.

As soon as he touched it, it was as if he'd been slapped hard in the face. Staggering back from the feeling, he sat there watching the building as something rose from the ground in front of it and stood before him. Finn quickly got onto his knees and bowed his head to show he'd meant no harm.

"There is darkness inside my walls, young dragon. You have awakened it." He told her he was sorry to have disturbed it. "I will allow it to you if you were to clear the darkness from within. It has been there for more years than I can remember now."

"I am a young dragon, my lady, but I will do whatever you wish to rid you of the darkness. It was only my intent to see how strong your walls were, so I might decide to use it again." She told him her name was Shadow, the Watcher of the Dead. "I will admit to you I've yet to have heard of you. I'm sorry for it as well."

"Rise up, Red Dragon, and let me have a look at your worth." Theo and his faerie came out of the first building, and Theo got down on his knees as well. "I've not seen dragons around for many years. I thought them all to be gone but a few. The Manning Dragons, as a matter of fact."

"We're sons of Xavier Manning, brother to the king and queen." She bowed before them. "Tell us what it is you need, my lady, and we'll take care it is fixed for you. So long as there will be no consequences other than the ones we have agreed upon."

"I wish for the darkness to be taken from my body here in this building. Once it happens, I will be free to help you for so long as you need me." Theo asked her what she would wish in return. "You are smart to ask. But all I wish is to be set free. To be able to work with such dragons as yourself, it will be my pleasure."

Finn didn't want to fuck this up. He didn't know why, but he thought if he simply released her, he'd be releasing more than just Shadow. Reaching for Dawn, the lady of the earth, he told her where he was and what creature was with him.

Hello, my dragon friend. How are you – ? I see you have found Shadow, Watcher of the Dead. She is mostly harmless. What is it she asks of you? He told her what she'd said, and tried very hard to remember what it was he'd said to her, the wording of his promise. Dawn laughed. *You are much smarter than even you think you are, Finn, the Red Dragon. Yes, you are smart to tell her she cannot harm others if you were to release her. I don't know she would, to be honest with you. As she has said, it has been a great many years since she has been heard of.*

He looked at the lady before him. She was beautiful, he thought. And while he didn't completely trust her, Finn prided himself on being able to word promises so any loopholes would mostly be covered.

"I shall release you from your burden so long you keep your promise to me that no one, magical or human, will be hurt by your magic. We've been sent here to take care the area is built up. I won't allow you or anyone else to take any more from the creatures living here." She stood there, her face as serene as Dawn's was when he spoke to her. When Shadow smiled at him, he wasn't sure if he should be relieved or more frightened.

"You have called on Dawn, Queen of the Earth. I hadn't any idea you knew her. I should have, you being a dragon. She has warned me as well that she will hunt me down should I harm you or her dragons. You have captured her eye and heart like no other, Finn, Red Dragon." He glanced at his brother, hoping he knew what she meant. "You free me, and I will do everything within my powers to not just help you in your tasks, but I shall also be beholden to you for the rest of your life."

"Then, I shall release you." She nodded and asked him to enter the building. Turning to his brother, he thought about the consequences of doing this if she wasn't on the up and up. "Theo, she said there is darkness in her body. I'm not at all sure what that means exactly, but keep your cell phone ready in case we need to call the police."

"I'll be right here. I won't leave you."

Finn entered the building and carefully sought out where he was supposed to go. He'd never released anyone before. He heard Theo tell him he'd called Dad too, just in case. Whatever it might mean, Finn thanked him.

"Do you see it there? The coldness seeping into my body?" Before he touched it, he asked her why it was her body and not the building that needed healing. "Ah, yes, you are very wise. It is because I was buried here by magic long before this building was created. Should you heat the stone there at the fireplace, I'll be released to help you. And I shall help you, Finn. I swear this to you on the heart of my own child."

Putting his hands to the stone surrounding the fireplace, Finn thought of all the heat it would have taken from the fireplace to have helped the woman. Letting his heat move from his hands to the stone, he could feel the letting go of something strong. For the life of him, Finn had no idea why he'd agreed to this. As soon as the stone, just a small one in the corner of the mantel, broke off and hit the floor, he felt a power and strength enter him he'd never felt before.

Thrown back, he hit his head and body hard on the wall. Trying to stand upright again, he saw moving colors dizzily moving around in his sight, and he couldn't make heads or tails of them. Closing his eyes, he opened them again when something slapped him in the face. Finn looked up at Theo and smiled. After that, he closed them again to allow his poor noddle, as his mom called his head, to rest.

~~~

Just as Rachel was putting the dishes in the rack near the

salad bar, she staggered back and fell against the wall behind her. Dishes went flying, and she knew she was going to get cut when some of the larger pieces of the dishware hit her on the legs and arms. She was still sitting on the floor where she'd fallen when her manager and sister-in-law came out to see what had happened.

"I don't know. I was putting the dishes in the slot there to help out in the kitchen, and all of a sudden, the floor started to heave, and I fell back. Did you feel it?" Sandra told her she'd not felt anything but had heard the crash. "Surely someone felt it. It knocked me on my butt just now."

"Rachel, do you have any idea how much this is going to cost me?" She looked at Sandra with a frown. "I know you've been here forever, but I'm going to have to write you up for this. Your brother is going to be really pissed off about this."

"You're joking, right?" Sandra told her she wasn't. "You're going to write me up because I dropped about five dishes? Are you flipping serious right now? There isn't any way you can do that. Not to me."

"I'm going to do it."

With a lift of her chin, Sandra left her there on the floor. She'd not even asked her if she was all right—just made her flipping announcement and left her there. Looking at the mess she'd made, which really wasn't all that bad, Rachel wondered why over the last few days, Sandra gotten such a burr up her butt.

Rachel picked up the glass and piled it on the tray nearby. Thinking about her friend, she really did wonder what was wrong with her—this time. Looking up when someone drew near to help her, Rachel smiled at Tommy.

"You hurt?" She told him not too much. "I got me some Band-Aids in my pack. Momma told me I have to carry them all the time. I can give you some of them if you give me some back. Can I have the ones with the green man on them?"

"Yes. I'll pick you up some, Tommy. I don't need any Band-Aids. I'm going home anyway soon. But I do thank you." He grinned at her, and she laughed. "You're just too nice to me. What will I do if you ever find another job? Be lost, I think."

Tommy Archer was handicapped, and more than likely the most loyal and friendly person who worked at the restaurant. He was nearly forty years old, but he had the mental capacity of about a ten year old. His parents had done a wonderful job with him, and he could hold down a menial job like bussing tables for the restaurant. Rachel thought her mom had hired him before her and Dad had passed away.

After getting the glass all picked up, she went to the kitchen to inspect her wounds. There were a lot of them, mostly superficial, but there were one or two she thought would need stitches. Limping to her locker after clocking out, she was in her car and driving home when she thought of the earth literally moving under her feet.

Why hadn't Sandra felt it? Why hadn't anyone else commented on it when she'd gone back to the kitchen? It wasn't as if something like that happened every day. Pulling into her driveway, her phone was ringing, and she could see it was the restaurant. Knowing it was Sandra, she declined the call and then turned off her phone.

If she was going to write her up, then so be it. Rachel didn't like working for the restaurant anymore anyway. Her brother owned a small percentage of it since their parents were gone, but Rachel owned the bulk of it. Rachel knew, too, that Sandra was forever cutting hours to make the payroll. The guidelines had been set up by their parents, and it didn't look to her like Sandra was following any of them. Rachel knew with her part of the inheritance from her parents, she could do a great many things.

After taking a long hot shower and getting dressed, she looked at her wounds again. They weren't nearly as bad as she'd first thought they were. The smaller ones were already healing up, and the two larger cuts were scabbing over. Good. One less thing she'd have to mess with.

Rachel had always been able to heal quickly. Her parents had told her that since she'd been old enough to understand she'd been adopted. They'd also told her she wasn't entirely human. Mom had always told her she more than likely had some shifter blood in her. Whatever the reason, she'd never been sick a day in her life, nor had she had any broken bones.

The pounding at her door had her telling them to back off. Chad, her brother, told her to let him in. She asked him what he wanted through the door. She could see him through the peephole and knew he was pissed off.

"Let me in, Rach. I'm not shitting you. I just got off the phone with Sandra, and she said you left your shift." Opening the door, she put her hand in front of him when he started to enter. "You want to do this out here? Fine. I'm supposed to fire you. She said you destroyed several hundred dollars' worth of dishes, and then just left."

"I do hope she's figured out there is no way to fire me since I'm the owner of the place. Are you here to get my side of the story or to yell at me? And just so you know, Chad, you'd better pick wisely. I'm no more in the mood for this shit than you are." He let out a long breath and asked her what had happened. "Thank you. The floor seemed to have shifted under my feet, and I broke six plates. If those are hundreds of dollars, then we're charging way too little for the food we put on them."

"Are you hurt?" She told him it was healing nicely. "Sandra has this thing about you lately that even I don't understand. Can I come in?"

She moved back so he could enter. "I don't understand her either. Since the two of you got married, and since Mom and Dad were killed, it's been like this train wreck between the two of us. I really only broke a few dishes. Then she said she was going to write me up. Chad, she can't do that. I own more of the place than you do. If she does that, I'm going to fucking fire her." She let out a breath too to calm herself. "I'm sorry. I'm trying very hard not to curse, and twice now I have. What is going on at home with you two? You don't have to tell me anything personal, all right? But there has to be something."

"I couldn't tell you—as in, I really have no idea. I mean, right now, I would tell you if I understood. And you're right, since we were married, it's been hell even being around her. Even for me. Yesterday I was sitting on the couch, and she came in there screaming at me about having to go someplace. I was trying my best to be calm, but she didn't want to hear it. I finally just pulled on my shoes and got in the car. By the time we got to the dinner party she swears she had told me about, it was as if nothing had happened. I don't know if I can take much more of her." He flopped down on the couch, kicking off his shoes. "I don't know what to do right now. She'll just bitch at me if I don't fire you. Something about taking your side all the time.

But if you leave, the restaurant is going to have worse sales than it does already because you aren't there to cook. I know you could work anywhere, Rach, but the place was Mom and Dad's baby."

Inviting him to stay for pizza, she ordered it while he called Sandra. Rachel heard him telling her he was with her now, and they were talking about their options. The only one she could see working right now was for her to quit or to fire Sandra. Either way, no one was going to be happy with the end results. Especially Chad, who seemed to be caught in the middle every time she and Sandra fought. Going back into the living room when he was no longer talking, she sat across from him on the couch.

"You have to tell me everything. I have a feeling you're stressing out too on some of the things she's been bitching at you about." Chad nodded. "Tell me. I think I need to know what I'm up against. Not to mention what you've been dealing with. I didn't do anything to her."

"I know that." He leaned back and closed his eyes before speaking. "It's everything about you. This house is larger than ours. I told her you'd bought it a long time ago and have been doing the improvements all along to make it look this good, but she says you're rubbing the fact that our home is smaller than yours in her face. We drive around in a five year old car. I have no idea what it means. Your car is almost as old as you are."

She laughed. "She really is jealous? I don't understand. We were okay, not really friends, but okay, hanging out together before you married her." Chad told her there was more. "Do I even want to know what else she thinks of me?"

"She thinks I got a bum deal when our parents died. I should sue you for your half of the estate." He didn't even move as tears started to fall down his cheeks. "I tried telling her I was a piece of shit when I was a teenager, and I knew Mom and Dad were going to take the money they had to pay out for damages as well as drug rehabilitation, but she won't hear it. Sandra says you're not really my sister anyway, and you should have shit. I can't tell you how much that hurts me, Rach. You *are* my sister."

It hurt her too. Her entire body ached with what Sandra thought of the relationship between her and Chad. Not his sister? They'd grown up together. They were sister and brother not by blood, but because they were brought together by their parents. Pushing back the pain for a moment, she cleared her throat. It wasn't working to make her feel better, so she got up and went to the kitchen, hoping Chad would give her a moment to collect herself. She smiled when she saw him.

"I have an idea." Rachel pulled out a bottle of wine when Chad joined her at the kitchen table. "You can tell me if it will work or not because I'm not going to bite your head off. But this is something I've been thinking about for a few days now."

"I'm assuming it's because of the way Sandra has been treating you. Not to mention, this conversation we're having right now." She told him not all of it, but some. "I'm so sorry about this, Rach. I truly am. I just don't know what is wrong with her."

"I'm not sure either, other than jealously, but I don't care for the way she's putting you in the middle. I wish if she had something to say about me she'd come to talk to me. But that's neither here nor there. I'm going to quit, or you're going to 'fire' me. Either way makes it so you're not in trouble at home." He said the restaurant would fail. "I can't work with her anymore,

Chad. You have to see it too. If the place fails, I'll just take it over, without her there, and start fresh. It's the only thing I can think of to make this work out for you and her."

"I'm sorry." She looked at him, and he said it again. "I just don't know what to do anymore, Rach. This is hurting all of us."

"Chad, I love you dearly, so don't get hurt by this. You need to stand up and tell your wife to shut the fuck up about me. I'm not the bad guy in all of this." He nodded. "I'm not joking. I have to think some of this is on you too, you not standing up to her about me being your sister. Did you tell her you weren't going to sue me, or is there something I need to look to happen?"

"I told her I'd think about it." She got up and poured her wine into the sink. Rachel had thought she was hurt before, but it wasn't even close to what she was feeling right now. "I'm not going to do it. But I don't know what to say to her."

"I think you should leave here." He asked her what she'd said. "It's time you left, Chad. I have nothing more to say to you if you don't know what to say to your wife, who is pounding a steel wedge between the two of us. I've forever had your back on everything you did. Even getting into trouble for you when you were in trouble. But this? You've shoved me down the river without any kind of support. Please go home to your wife. If you're going to sue me, I'd like to know as soon as you decide. I've not the energy nor the heart to try and talk to you right now."

She waited for the sound of the door to close behind him before she let go of her hurt. Crying, sobbing with the pain he'd given her, Rachel slid to the floor and curled into a tight ball and let it all out. She didn't even try to hold anything back as she lay there. Her brother. Rachel was going to lose her brother over this, and she had no idea what to do about it.

When the pizza arrived, she paid for it and tipped the young man. She knew she looked a wreck but didn't care. Taking the pizza to the kitchen, Rachel tossed it into the trash. Her hurt was too great, and eating right now would have made her sick.

Going to her bedroom, she packed up a few things she might need and decided she was going to take the first plane out of there. Not caring where she ended up, she tossed her passport in the bag as well.

Rachel was halfway to the door when she felt dizzy, her body heavy. Holding onto the couch back, she was sick. Something was wrong with her head, and it hurt like someone had taken a hammer to it a couple of times. Something or someone was hurting her. Going to her knees to make sure she didn't fall back and hit her head again — if that was what had happened — Rachel let the darkness take her under, terrified she'd not be found lying dead on the floor for a month.

Chapter 3

"Finn? Finn? Are you all right?" Opening his eyes, he looked at the person standing over him, not having any idea who it might be. "It's Dover. You knocked yourself pretty hard when you were tossed back from whatever it was. Right now, you're lying in the yard behind the house. The rest of us have been scared out of our minds. What the fuck was that?"

"I don't know. Let me sit up for a minute." He was helped up, his body seemingly weak from whatever had happened. "I don't know what happened. I mean, I did fall when I was freeing Shadow, but I got up from that, right?"

"Yes. You said you were fine, only shaken up a little bit. Do you remember that?" Things were starting to come back to him now, and he nodded. Holding his head when he did that, he told Dover he remembered. "Then what happened? You didn't say much other than you hurt. When asked why, all you said was, Chad broke your heart. Who the fuck is Chad?"

"There was a woman." Dover told him there wasn't a

woman. "No, not here, but when I was out. I didn't see her face, not clearly, but I did see her. Chad is her brother. I think. I'm not clear on that because from some of the argument I heard between the two of them, it wasn't clear if he was or not. I'm confused."

"*You're* confused? How do you think we feel? You were just coming out of the building, looking like you'd conquered the world, then you stopped moving, clutched your heart, said something about a man breaking your heart, then fell forward. You hit your head on a rock over there and broke it—not your head like one would think, but the rock. What the fuck is going on with you?" Finn thought about the conversation he'd overheard. "Finn? You're scaring me right now."

"Just listen to me for a minute. When I released Shadow, I watched a part of the fireplace break off. A smallish stone or something. It was strange the way it just seemed to float to the floor. When it hit, it was like you see on television when a sonic boom is going on. The waves flow out from the source. Anyway. Then I heard this woman's voice, talking to a person about her legs being cut from some dishes. The dishes were broken because of the shifting of the ground. Like the rock hitting the floor had caused this tremor to happen around her." Dover asked him if he knew if it was a dream or not. "I don't have any idea, but I don't think it was. She was as real as you and I are. But somehow, she was a part of what I was doing here. Or I was a part of her life where she is. I'm not sure."

"Okay, let me get this straight. You think a woman you don't know was cut by the earth shifting under her feet when a rock here was knocked off the fireplace where you were just minutes ago. Not only that, but Chad someone, her brother, you think, has broken your heart? Or is it her heart? Either way, someone's heart was broken." Finn told him it was her heart. "Does it really matter right now?"

"I think it does. I have no idea why, but I think she's somehow connected to me and the releasing of Shadow." Dover shook his head and asked him what he'd been drinking. "I don't drink, and you know it. This is serious. This woman, whoever she is, we're connected, and I'd very much like to figure out how and why."

"All right. Let me see what I can find out with the information you've given me." Dover, forever with a computer pad with him, started typing on it with the information Finn gave him. "There are just too many variables, I'm afraid. I have some names here, but nothing really we can narrow down to help you."

"I'll ask Mom. Maybe she can make some sense of it."

Reaching for his mom, he had another thought. This time he didn't voice it to his brother. He was freaked out enough as it was. Mom was laughing when she answered his call. After explaining to her what had happened, she was quiet for some time.

I'm with your Aunt Carson. She's feeding in the information you have. As for why this connection happened, have you thought of the reasons for it? I mean, my mind is all over the place right now with it. Finn asked her if she meant the woman being his mate. *Yes. That's exactly it. How else would you be able to connect with a perfect stranger? Nor do you have any other information on her.*

Honestly? I don't know. I'm only trying to figure this out myself. She told him that she and his dad would be there in a couple of weeks to have a nice visit. *I'd love that. We'll cook out and have a nice day or two of it.*

Okay, here is what she said she can find. The woman is not too far from you. Her name is, Carson thinks, Rachel Merkel. Adoptive parents are both deceased. A brother named Chad Merkel, who has a record for when he was younger, but nothing now. Married to a woman by the name of Sandra Smart Merkel, who is currently managing the restaurant 'Merkel's Mark.' The restaurant is owned by Rachel and Chad, Carson said. Finn told her about the conversation he'd heard about her owning most of it. *I'd say that. Rachel owns ninety-seven percent. I'm not sure of the other three, it doesn't say here. Oh, wait. Her brother owns it—Chad Merkel. Just his name too. Not the wife, for some reason. Also, this is very strange. The restaurant is losing money hand over fist. I wonder what is going on there. It's been losing money for a few months now. But a great deal of it in the last eight weeks.*

I don't think she's aware of that. At least that's nothing she brought up with her brother. Mom told him she didn't think she was aware of it either. *What else can you tell me? Like, how close are we talking? I need…. I have no idea why, but I have this very strong urge to go and see if she's all right.*

Let me see. She was adopted by the Merkels when she was an infant. It was done through legal channels. She's smart. Invests well. Owns her own home. A nice one she paid very little for, as you told me. Rachel has been working on it over the years since she purchased it, and it's worth a great deal more than she paid for it. Carson is looking for a picture of her now. Finn told his mom he didn't want to see it. *Why not? Don't you want to see if she stirs up anything in you?*

I don't. I have no idea why, but I actually feel a little guilty about the information you've given me so far. Mom said he was a good boy. *Thanks, Mom. But it's doubtful she'd feel that way if she figured out I was sort of spying on her.*

Here is the address. It wasn't far from where he was, less than ten miles. *Also, this is something else you should be aware of. She's not human. Her parents knew when she was adopted, but it doesn't look as if she was ever tested as to what she could be.*

When I overheard her conversation with Chad, she did say she was healing nicely. I didn't put it together with her ability to heal quickly. But it makes sense now that I put it in the context. Mom told him there was more. *I have enough to check on her now. And to know she's not going to freak out if I am her mate. Or maybe she's the freak out kind of person. I'll let you know what I find out.*

After making sure the building was secure, and his brothers knew where he was headed, Finn made his way to his car. He wasn't going to barge into her life right now, but he really did want to make sure she was all right. He'd fallen. There was no telling what that might have done to her if they really were connected somehow.

The neighborhood was one of those places having a resurgence of homes. Of the ten or so on the street Rachel lived on, it looked as if nine of them were currently being worked on. The address he had for Rachel put her in the mid-section of the street, and her home was the best looking on the block. Finn also thought it was what had inspired the other people on the street to get their homes in better shape.

Sitting in his car, Finn looked up at the house. Watching as the mailman walked to the house, ringing the doorbell, he was surprised when no one answered his call. Getting out just as the man left the package on the step, he saw her car was there, and the garage door was still open. Going to the back yard so no one would be suspicious of him, he sat down on the patio deck chair and tried reaching into the house and to Rachel.

"Hello? Rachel?" He could feel her pain and worried about it for a moment. *Rachel, honey, are you all right?*

Who's there? Finn was so relieved to hear from her he had to sit there for a moment to let himself absorb how wonderful he felt. *Who the fuck is this? Why are you in my house?*

My name is Finn. I'm not in your home but on your back patio. I guess technically I'm in your home, but I was worried about you. He felt her dealing with her pain. *I think we're connected somehow. You were hurt when I was. I came here to make sure you're all right.*

Why the fuck would you think – ? My fucking head feels like it's going to come off my shoulders. If you really are out on my deck, come in through the garage. I think it's still open, and I'm in the hallway towards the front of the house. Fuck, my head is killing me. He did what she told him, concerned with how she'd allow him, a stranger, to come into her home. *I'm sick.*

Running now, he picked her up in his arms, asking for directions to the bathroom. Getting her in there was no easy feat, as she was really sick, and the room was tiny. After sitting her on the floor, making sure she was all right, he stepped into the hallway and stripped down and used his magic to redress without her seeing him. She'd already been sick on him, and he didn't want her to feel bad because of it. Finn could hear her emptying her belly over and over until she just laid on the floor in front of the commode.

She turned enough to look at him with one eye but stayed on the floor where he'd put her. Sitting on the floor outside the door so she could see him better, he asked her if she was all right.

"I have no idea. I've never had a headache like this before. What did you do to me?" Finn explained to her as best he could about what he'd done and how he'd felt her. "For now, I guess I'll let that go. But it's so full of holes I could literally see you through it."

"I understand. Do you need anything? You didn't sound as if you had that much on your stomach." Rachel told him about the pizza she'd thrown away, but nothing more. "You should eat a little something. I'm not sure how it worked out, but I'm thinking you have a concussion. From when I fell."

"That makes no sense at all. You understand that, don't you?" Finn told her he knew. "How did you find me? I'm assuming you saw something that led you here. What was it?"

"Not so much what I saw, which was very little, but what I heard. You and your brother had an argument. You kicked him out over what his wife believes about you." Rachel sat up but didn't move out of the bathroom. "I haven't any idea what has happened to make it so I can hear the things you say. I don't suppose you could hear anything I was saying?"

"You were working to free someone. I only just realized it wasn't thoughts in my head. Dover. Someone was there named Dover, and he was giving you a hard time because you broke a rock." She looked at him. "This seems weird and out there, but I think you're a dragon." Finn told her he was. "Okay. I don't know where to go with that. You're really a dragon?"

"I am. A red dragon. Very rare. Would you like to see him?" She assured him now was not the time. "I suppose you're right. This hallway would be sorely damaged if I had to shift right now."

She eyed him, and he had to laugh. "I suppose you think

just because I allowed you into my house to save me from cleaning up puke that we're the best of buds, don't you?" He told her he only wanted to make sure she was all right. "Sure. And now that I have puke breath, you'd just as soon leave me here rather than raping and pillaging me."

Finn couldn't help it, he laughed again. "I'm not sure how one goes about pillaging a woman, but I suppose it could be done. However, I want you to know that number one, I can't lie to you. I promise you, Rachel, I'm here only to make sure you're all right."

"Wait. What you said right there means something. It means— I'm not entirely sure, but I've heard it before. Something about shifters not— Christ, you don't think I'm going to be related to you, do you?" Finn wouldn't have lied to her anyway, but he honestly told her he had no idea if they were mates or not. "That's it. Mates. You so don't want to be my mate, Mr.... I've forgotten your name."

"Finn. Manning is my last name. Why wouldn't I want to be your mate? Other than the puke breath, of course." When she growled at him, Finn laughed again. "You're adorable. I want you to know that right away, in a sort of mean streak kind of way. How are you feeling? I want to make sure you have something to eat before you show me my walking papers."

"I'm capable of fixing myself something to eat if I want it." Finn nodded, then stood up. "Where are you going? Why are you being so nice right now? Agreeable and shit like that?"

"As you said, you're all right, and you can cook yourself something to eat. I was thinking I'd like to take you to dinner. A nice steak meal with all the trimmings sounds good to me. However, I can understand, with a headache, you might not want to go out." Her belly growled, and he heard it. Choosing to ignore it, for now, he leaned against the wall in front of the little room. "The only way I can tell if you're my mate is to smell you. As you might have guessed or might know, I can't do that with all the other scents in the room. Being agreeable? I like to think I can be when I'm not pushed into a corner. Some people, even knowing I'm a dragon, think I can be pushed and pushed. But they soon learn I'm a good deal smarter and stronger than most. What are you?"

"A woman. I know what you're asking me, and I'm not trying to push you into anything, but that's all I know about myself. I was adopted into this family." Finn told her he knew that. "How did you figure out I'm not wholly human?"

"In one of the conversations you were having, someone asked you how you were doing, and you told them the wounds from the glass were healing. My mom, who is a wonderful woman, pointed it out to me. My aunt works for the government, and that's how I figured out where it is you live."

"This is all very strange, you know." He agreed with her. When she stood up too, he didn't back from her when she came into the hall with him. "You're very tall, aren't you? I mean, there aren't too many people taller than I am."

"I would guess not." Finn inhaled, trying his best not to let her see he was working to get her scent. When she grinned at him, he didn't know what to think. "I don't know what you think is funny, but you're my mate, Rachel."

"I figured it out as well. I'm not sure how I did other than smelling you. You smell homey and comforting. Like something I need near me, or I'll die. Is that about right?" Finn nodded. "I would like to have dinner with you. But no funny stuff. My head doesn't hurt as bad as it did, but it's still a little fuzzy."

"I'd love that. Would you feel more comfortable having dinner with me and my brothers, or just you and me?" Rachel told him just him this time. "Works for me. If you want to get ready, or just wear what you have on, I'm ready anytime you are."

"I have to change and brush my teeth." Neither of them moved. "How many brothers do you have, Finn Manning? I have just the one."

"Five of them. And five uncles and my dad are married to wives that are kick ass. They scare even them. May I kiss you, Rachel?" She shook her head and said she still had puke breath. "Oh. All right. Later then."

When she left him there to race up the stairs, he slid down the wall and let out a long breath. Holy fuck balls, he'd found his mate. And she was going to be eaten alive by his mom and the aunts. Damn, but he wished right now he'd been born an only child with no one to take her to meet. Then he grinned. Well, perhaps they'd be nice to her the first time they met her. A man could hope, couldn't he?

~~~

Her cell phone was ringing when she got to the bottom of the stairs—Rachel hadn't taken it up with her to change and to brush her teeth. She was happy Finn hadn't answered it, but he was holding it out to her when she stood in front of him. The picture was of Sandra, and she wasn't sure if she should answer it. Rachel was in too good of a mood to have her sister-in-law ruin it.

"I'll be right here if you need me. I know a little more than you do about the restaurant. As I said, my aunts and mom work for the government."

Rachel asked him if Sandra was stealing money. With his nod, she answered the phone.

"What do you want, Sandra? I'm in no mood to put up with your bullshit right now. I have a date, and we're going to have some fun." Putting the phone on speaker, she didn't care at all if Finn heard what Sandra told her. Rachel wanted to talk to her about the money she'd been missing anyway. Sandra told her they were going to hash this out. "No. As I said, I'm just on my way out."

"All right. I'll be blunt with you. I don't want you to come back to work. Ever. I've spoken to my husband, and we've decided that we're going to sue you for the estate. He should have had it all in the first place. I'm not even sure why you were entitled to any of it." Rachel looked up at Finn, who picked her up and took her to the living room. After putting her on the couch, he sat across from her in the chair. "Did you hear me?"

"I did. I'm trying to think why you are telling me this and not my brother." Sandra said that he wasn't her brother. "Ah, but he is. I have all the paperwork that says we're related. His parents adopted me—"

"I don't care what you think you might have. I'm sick of you getting the better end of the estate. Not to mention everything else that shouldn't be yours in the first place. I should have had it." Rachel asked her if she meant Chad should have had it. "Whatever. We're a unit, he and I. And you should just give up now on trying to keep us from doing this."

"Where is Chad?" Sandra asked her why would she care where he was. "Because he's my brother. How many times do I have to repeat myself before you realize that we're related and that the will has been finalized? Chad knows why he didn't get his full estate. You should talk to him. After I get to."

"I told him I never wanted him to talk to you again. And because he loves me, he's decided I'm the smarter of the two of us." When the doorbell rang, Finn got up to get it. Whoever it was, they were shitting on her day, and she didn't like it. Finn entered the room with Chad just as Sandra was speaking again. "Chad and I have agreed that you're worthless and that you have no rights to anything his parents left you. It's a shame they didn't see you as we have since they've passed away."

"And how do you figure I'm not entitled to anything they left me? You and Chad had only been married for what—a month when they passed away?" Chad put his finger to his lips, showing, she supposed, for her not to tell Sandra he was there. "Why don't you explain to me the conversation you and Chad had about me being sued by the two of you for everything my parents left me?"

"Like I'm going to tell you what we're going to say at the hearing. You should just give it up now, Rachel. There is no way in hell you're going to win against a biological child of the people that took you in, for pity sake." Rachel looked at her brother and noticed he was upset. Well, he'd better not be pissy with her. "Rachel, are you fucking listening to me?"

"Yes, as a matter of fact, I am. Before we get to whatever you want and your suing me, I'd like to ask you where the money is going from the receipts at Merkel's." Sandra's silence was very telling to her. "I've been going over the books once you leave for the day. Several hundred thousand dollars are missing from the last four—"

"You stay the fuck out of my office. Wait until I tell Chad

you're fucking with the deposits. He'll finally see you for what you truly are." She laughed, maniacal and sounding desperate too. "So what if there is money missing from the deposits? It's not like it's yours anyway. It should have been ours all along. You can just think of it as me making sure I have what should have come to me in the first place."

"That's the second time you've said 'I' when talking about what Chad should be getting. It sounds to me like this entire thing—suing me, taking the money, and cooking up the books—is more about you than the two of you. What do you have to say about that?" Sandra said nothing. "Now, I have to ask you if you're listening to me."

"I deserve a great deal for marrying that sap. Christ, he can't even satisfy me in bed enough that I don't have to go and find someone else to help me through sex. Do you have any idea what sort of idiotic things he says about you? It's almost as if he loves you more than he does me." Rachel watched Chad. She had a moment where she thought he already knew what his wife thought of him. "Once I take care of you, I'm going to do the same to him. I should have wondered why I never had to sign a prenup with the idiot. There wasn't going to be anything for us to inherit when his parents died."

"Chad should hear you now, Sandra. I think he'd be surprised at what a vicious bitch you are." Sandra laughed and said that he was aware of it now. "Are you telling me that you only married him because you thought there was going to be money? That's not right. In fact, that's just terrible."

"Oh, grow up, you moron. Everyone does it. I bet even when you marry, the man stupid enough to align himself with you is going to be broke as fuck and want everything you have. Won't he be surprised to find out that I'm going to take it all from you, and you'll have jack shit." Looking at Finn, she laughed when he mouthed that he had more than enough money for both of them if that happened. "What do you find so fucking funny now, you cunt? Christ, I hate you. I have loathed you since the first time I laid eyes on you and found out you were related to that sap I was planning to take to the cleaners."

Finn ran his finger over his throat, and Rachel decided she liked the idea of hanging up on Sandra. Closing the connection, he handed her his cell phone. When she asked him what it was for, Finn fiddled with it for a few seconds, and the room exploded with the sounds of Sandra talking. The sounds sent peels of laughter not only from her but Chad as well.

"What happened at your home, Chad? I'm assuming the two of you had a huge fight." When Chad glanced at Finn, not answering her, she smiled. "This is my mate, Finn Manning. He is taking the two of us out to dinner tonight, and we're going to have a nice conversation with him and his brothers. If he can get them to come. I have a feeling we're going to need as much back up from them as we can get. By the way, he's a dragon."

When they shook hands, she got up to stretch. Leaving the two of them in the living room, she went to the bathroom. Rachel just needed a minute to gather herself. The things Sandra had said to her hurt her heart to the core. She could only imagine the things she'd said to Chad to have brought him to her door. Washing her face and running a quick brush through her hair, she figured she was as ready as she could be. Coming out of the room, she saw Chad standing there waiting for her.

"I'm so sorry, Rach." She nodded and hugged him back when he pulled her into his arms. "I've left her. I don't think she heard that part when I stormed out of the house, but I can't live with her anymore. I want you to know, too, I hadn't any idea she was stealing money from the restaurant. I'll make sure it's returned to you."

"Don't worry about it. Okay? I'm just glad this is coming out now, and you're going to be all right. You are, aren't you, Chad?" He said it was difficult, but he was going to make it. "You can stay here with me. The house is certainly big enough, as Sandra pointed out."

They were both laughing as they made their way to the front door. Finn was there, and when he smiled at her, she felt the warmth of it all the way to her toes. Taking his hand into hers when it was offered, Rachel sat in the front seat with Finn as Chad rode in the back.

"My brothers are going to meet us there. I hope you don't mind, but I've told my mom what was going on with Sandra as well. They'll take care that nothing happens to either of you while she's out there making trouble." Rachel asked if she thought she would. "I would count on it, especially after she finds out that Chad is living here with you. You will, won't you? It might be the safest place for the two of you right now."

"She already asked me, and I think you're right." Chad told them both he was sorry. "I never realized any of the things she said today. None of it. But when I think back on things, especially after my parents died, I can see things that I never thought of before. Like the extra money she always claimed she had. I've never seen any of it. I haven't any idea where it might have gone either."

"As I said, don't worry about it. We'll get through this, and things will be the way they should have been." Chad said he didn't think it would ever be again. "Well then, they'll be as normal as we can make them. Is that better?"

When they pulled up in front of the restaurant, Rachel was startled by the size of the men that hugged Finn. Their poor mom must be nuts to have had more children after the first one was born. And she'd find out, apparently. Their parents were on their way here tomorrow to meet her and her brother. Rachel was suddenly terrified of making a good impression.

Then she realized she didn't care if they liked her or not. She was who she was, and they'd better not say a word to her. Laughing to herself, she wondered what a dragon would do to her if they didn't like her. Whatever it was, things were about to get real for Sandra Merkel. And for the life of her, Rachel couldn't make herself feel sorry for the other woman.

Chapter 4

Sandra loved having the house to herself. She had no idea where moron had gone, but she didn't care at this point. Things were beginning to progress the way they should have a long time ago, and she was happy for it. Even not having any money tonight didn't bother her overly much. Soon she'd have that big house Rachel had, and things would be perfect.

Just as she was turning off the television, having watched all the programs she wanted, her cell phone rang. She didn't know why the police were contacting her at nine at night, but she hoped it was to tell her that Rachel had been killed in some terrible way. Answering it with a hopeful heart, the officer asked her to state her name and address, please. For verification.

"Mrs. Merkel, this is to inform you that the restaurant Merkel's Mark has been closed down as of closing time tonight." She asked him what the hell he was talking about. "I'm getting there. As of this evening, after all the employees were clocked out and gone for the night, the owners of the restaurant closed the doors until further notice. I'm also to tell you that your keys no—"

"What the fuck are you talking about? I own that place. I've been running it for years." He asked her if she did indeed own it, or only ran it. "It's the same thing. I'm the one in charge. No one is going to change any locks on it either if that was what you were going to tell me. I'm telling you right now, if the locks have been changed without my permission, I'm going to be owning your pension and everything else you bought with your blood money."

"Mrs. Merkel, if you have solid proof that you are the sole owner of the restaurant, then we'll gladly hand you the keys. But Ms. Rachel Merkel is the owner, with her fiancé, and they have shut it down. As of right now, the place is closed indefinitely." Her head was hurting, she was so angry. "Do you have any questions for me at this time?"

"Yes, I want to know who the fuck you think you are for closing up something that doesn't belong to anyone but me." The officer told her he didn't have anything showing she owned even a percentage of it. "My husband does. And he's not going to be happy with what this woman has done. You are to open it back up right now, or so help me, I'm going to go down there and make you."

"I'm not terribly worried about what you may or may not be doing to me, Mrs. Merkel. I have it on good authority that things will not be going your way in the very near future, so you might want to get used to this feeling." He laughed, and she saw red, she was so pissed. "You have a good evening now."

Slamming the phone down on the table, she was pissed even more when not only did her phone break, but the table did as well. Cheap shit. That's all she'd been able to get since marrying the moron, cheap shit to have in this equally cheap house.

Having no way to call Rachel to ask her what was going on, she decided to make her way to the restaurant. If her key didn't work, she was going to make sure she shoved her keys up the ass of that fucking bitch. Going to the garage, she pulled open the door to find that her fucking car was gone. Chad had taken her only means of transportation.

"Mother fuck." If felt pretty good to be able to scream. But it did her little good in getting things to go her way. It wasn't that far, but walking to the place in the middle of the night was dangerous. Then she smiled. Dangerous for who? Certainly not her in the mood she was in.

Walking did help her to cool off a little. Not that she couldn't ramp up her mood again, but for now, she was calmer. As soon as she got to Merkel's, she did indeed get pissed off again. The cops were still there, and they looked as if they were having a grand party.

Going up to the first one that turned her way, she drew back to punch him in the face. It was the voice, the low voice behind her, that not only had her stopping her flying fist but turning slowly toward the man.

"You must be the famed Sandra Merkel. If you hit that man, not only will you end up in jail for the rest of the night, but perhaps into the morning. Certainly, until the judge decides to see you. Why are you here?" She asked him what his part in this was. "My part? I guess you could say that I have a vested interest in this place. My brother and future sister-in-law own it. My name is Theo Manning."

"What sister-in-law? And why should I give a shit why you think it should matter to me?" He told her who the woman was. "No. I don't think so. You'll have to come up with a better lie than that. Rachel isn't going to marry anyone. First of all, she doesn't date. Secondly, she would have mentioned it to me had she found someone stupid enough to marry her. That's a lie, and you know it."

He shrugged. "Think what you like. I know I'm telling you the truth." Sandra wanted to hit him too, but she was slightly afraid of his size. "You'd do well to get your ass back to your home and wait until you're summoned. You will be too, I'm sure. But for now, I want to make you understand that this place, like the others, that Rachel and Chad own will be guarded by armed men, and you should consider them dangerous."

"Who the hell do you think you are, telling me stuff like this? Are you threatening me? If so, I'm going to have the police here arrest you for threatening me." The officer she'd planned to hit told her that Theo had not threatened her, but was giving her fair warning. "All you men here, what do you do when you're not threatening helpless women? Suck each other off? Sounds like something you'd all be doing."

Sandra knew she might have taken a step too far, but when they all laughed, she looked around. What the fucking hell did they think was so funny now? Stomping, making her way to the man who had threatened her, she looked him right in the eye. Well, as well as she could with him towering over her. Working up a little spit, she was ready to launch it when he smiled at her.

"You do, and it will be the very last thing you ever do in your very short and miserable life. I will kill you if you spit on me." There was no point in looking around for help. They were laughing again and telling the big powerful looking man to do it anyway. "That wasn't a fair warning or a threat. It was a promise. Would you like to test me on it?"

"You're going to pay for this." She had started back toward her house when she turned to the men there. "One of you needs to give me a ride home. It's late, and someone might want to harm me."

"If it were anyone that knew you, Mrs. Merkel, I would say there are any number of people out there that wish to hurt you." The officer, she didn't know his name, smiled at her as he went to the cruiser that was still in the parking lot. "If you'd like to have a seat, I'll be right with you. I just have to make a phone call."

"I'm right here. You're going to take me home right now or so help me, I'm going to own all your jobs." He asked her how she was planning to do that. "I'm going to call the mayor and tell him what a shitty job you've been doing here. Crime is at an all-time high."

"Actually, crime is down by fifteen percent since the Mannings moved to this area. I don't know the precise reasoning behind it, but we've not had so much as a pick and go at a garage sale. In the event you might not know, it means someone picked up an item that didn't belong to them and walked off with it." She told him she knew just what it meant. "Good. Like I said, other than what you've been up to, things have been pretty quiet around here."

"What do you mean, what I've been up to?" No one said a word. "I asked you a question. What do you mean by that statement? I've done nothing illegal. Not one thing."

"Are you ready to go on home now?" She asked about the

phone call. "I got my answer. Things are set up now. You get in the back there, and I'll take you to where you came from."

Strange wording, but she didn't care. Right now, she needed a way to take care of some business. First of all, she needed to order a cell phone. Thinking about the list of things she had to do, Sandra wondered if she'd be able to get any sleep at all tonight. Looking at the clock on the dashboard, she couldn't believe it was well after two o'clock in the morning.

By the time they were pulling up in front of her house, she was fit to be tied, as her mother used to say. There wasn't a person who she could depend on to help her out of this mess, either. Especially not her husband. He was on her list too. Chad was going to figure out where his loyalties lie, and he'd better not be picking that awful woman, Rachel.

"Hello, Sandra." Startled, she looked up to see not just Rachel on her front porch, but Chad and some other man as well. "What's up? You here for any particular reason?"

"Yes. A better question would be, what the hell are you doing here? And Chad? Where the hell is my car? I went to use it when the police called me, and it was gone. I've told you a thousand times, we need a second car. That's the first thing we're buying when this mess is cleaned up. Me a new car." She pulled out her keys and went to the door. "You never answered me, Rachel. What the hell are you doing at my—our home at two in the morning?"

"Changing the locks." Sandra sort of heard what she said, something about locks, but her keys weren't working at the moment, so she didn't pay any attention to her. "It's not going to work, Sandra, no matter how much you fiddle with it. I told you, we changed the locks. Or Chad had them changed. There will be a—"

"Give me the key." Chad backed away from her, shaking his head. "Give me the fucking key, Chad. I'm not in any kind of mood to fuck with this tonight. I don't know where you get off changing the locks on anything, but this is my house, and I will not be locked out of it too."

"I don't want you in there." She just stared at him. "I've filed for divorce as well, Sandra. I'm not going to put up with your shit anymore. I heard what you said to Rach. I heard every word of it."

"So? What right does that give you to try and lock me from my home?" He said it wasn't hers anymore. "What the hell does that mean? Not that it matters. You're going to give me that key right now, or I'm going to knock the shit out of her, Chad. You know that I will too. I've done it to you before."

"You hit him? You hit my brother?" Sandra told Rachel to stay out of this. "You're a piece of work, aren't you? Not that it matters, but Chad sold the house to me tonight. It just so happens that I have friends in high places, and all the paperwork has been filed, and I'm the one that you have to deal with." Glaring at Chad, Sandra asked him why he'd do that to her. "I did it to you, Sandra. After talking to you and letting Chad hear all about how you didn't really care for him, we talked about a great many things. One of them being this house. You see, we don't trust that you'd do right by him, so we took matters into our own hands."

Turning to Rachel, she wondered what anyone could see in this woman. She was stiff as a board, unfriendly, and she didn't have a lick of sense. The man behind Rachel laughed. Sandra asked him what he thought was so funny.

"You. For a moment there, I thought you were thinking of yourself when you were describing the person in your head. But then I realized you were talking about Rachel here. She's beautiful, first of all. And the most friendly woman I've ever had the pleasure of falling in love with. Also, stiff? Not so much. Rachel has been very helpful to those she loves. I'm hoping with that statement, you understand she doesn't care all that much for you." Sandra asked him how he knew what she was thinking. "I would think that was obvious. I was reading your mind. Rachel will be able to do it as soon as she has more practice. I might even pass along that little bit of magic to Chad. I think he'd fare better if he knew just how people felt about him. Although, most people like him a great deal. You? Not so much."

"Like I care what people think about me. And I don't know how you were guessing my thoughts, but you stay away from me." The man told her he didn't have to be close to her to read her thoughts. "Stop that, you fucking bastard. My thoughts are my own. One of you is going to give me the keys to my home, or I'm going to call someone to come here and burn the place to the ground."

"Officer, you heard her. She threatened to burn down my sister's new home." Before she could even think what Chad was saying, she was cuffed up and on the back of the cruiser being searched. Sandra knew she was being felt up and struggled to get away from the man, but he only kicked her feet wider apart and finished molesting her. Turning around when he finished with her, she glared at the cop then looked at Chad. He was standing right in front of her. "You've bitten off more than you can chew, Sandra. I'm so glad I was able to see the little world you've made for yourself fall down around your ears."

"You're not going to divorce me, Chad. Do you want to know why?" He smiled and nodded at her. "Because you'd be fucking lost without me. Not only that, but you also don't have the balls to stand up to me in a courtroom. Because I plan on telling them every little detail about our sex life. I'll be telling them how you can't get it up most of the time, and that you just fuck like you're rocking a chair. In and out, in and out. No pleasure for me at all."

"Really? You're going to blame me for our sex life?" He leaned in close enough that she could hear his whisper. "It was you that kept me from having a hard on, Sandra. 'Do this.' 'Don't touch me there.' 'Get out of my way, and I'll do it myself.' It's hard to keep up with all your demands and have a hard on too while having you naked around me. You just keep on doing yourself right into prison." She was still screaming at him when she was put in the back of the cruiser again. "You have a nice night there, Sandra. Try very hard not to get into too much more trouble while you're in jail."

Sandra didn't know what was going on, but she was going to take care of it as soon as she got it figured out. Before they were out of the driveway to her home, the cop that was driving told her there would be an officer around the home and the restaurant until her trial was taken care of.

"What am I going to trial for?" He just laughed. "Fucking morons. You know that it's a sure sign of insanity when you laugh at things that aren't the least bit funny, don't you?"

It didn't stop him. He laughed off and on all the way to the station. As soon as they stopped and he got out of the car, several more cops came out of the building. They were surrounding her as if they were protecting her. She asked one of them who was out to get her.

"I would imagine a great many people, but we're here to make sure you don't escape. We were told that if you do, none of us would have a job come morning. Christ, you've shit in someone's oatmeal, haven't you?" She told him to shut up. "I see. Right there is what they were talking about. I guess I can understand why you're on the shit list now."

After being put into a cell with several other people, she was given a pillow, a sheet, and a blanket. They told her if she wanted, she could have a jumpsuit too. Not even bothering to answer the woman, she tossed the things on the little bed and sat on the floor. They'd get the message that she wasn't happy soon enough, Sandra figured. But when the officer laughed all the way back down the hall, Sandra wondered if everyone in this town had gone completely bonkers. Then it hit her.

"Where is that smell coming from?" Turning to look, she glared at the people standing or sitting behind her in the small space. "One of you has to have a bath. You're stinking up everyone's air. Christ. Was it you?"

Pointing to the nastiest woman in the cell, Sandra asked her again if it had been her. As soon as she stood up, Sandra knew she was going to teach a lesson or two here. The woman had to have been seven feet tall and weighed at least three hundred pounds. Not caring what happened to the other woman, Sandra stood up too. This was going to end badly. It was really too bad that it wasn't Chad or his sister that she was going to teach this lesson to. But she could pretend, she thought. Pretend and beat the shit out of this person.

~~~

Are you all right? Finn told his mom that he was better than ever. *I can understand that, I guess. How is your mate? I'm hoping you can tell me if I'm going to like her or not.*

I don't know why you'd not love her as much as I do. But yes, Mom, I think you'll like her a great deal. She told him she'd never had a daughter-in-law before. *Well, I guess the two of you have more in common than you thought. She's never had a mother-in-law before.*

Smartass. He watched their jet landing and told Rachel that they were here. *Your dad and uncles are happy that you've been taking care of things here. I just want you to know that I'm so very proud of all of my boys.*

I love you too, Mom. And you can talk to me in person when you get off the plane. You are planning to get off it, aren't you? She told him she was nervous. *So is Rachel, if that is any help. Chad is here as well. He's a little beaten up after last night, so be gentle with him. I feel for the man and the things his wife said to him.*

When she promised she'd be good but not to count on the others to behave, he laughed when they all—each of his uncles who were not already there, their wives, and the family attorney—got off the plane before his mom and dad.

"Holy fuck. They're all here." He kissed Rachel on the nose and made his way to the doors they'd be coming through. "I don't think this is a good idea. There are so many of them. What the hell were we thinking?"

"We were thinking that you should meet my family. I didn't know they were all coming either." She looked at him, and he laughed. "You look like you're ready to hit me. I'd not if I were you. My uncle is the king of dragons. He might not like it if you hit his favorite nephew."

"Are you? His favorite, I mean?" Finn just shook his head at Chad, who looked green. Finn said that they were all his favorites. It would depend on which one was closest to him at the time he said it as to who was the favorite at that time. "I see. My mom used to tell people I was her favorite male child. I never really thought it was funny then. But now, I think I'd give just about anything to have her say it to me one more time. What do you think she'd say about all this?"

"That she's glad you're happy?" Finn walked to the line of people coming through the gate while Rachel boosted her brother up. "That she's glad you finally grew a set of balls? I don't know, Chad. I think she'd be glad you were getting up off your ass and doing something productive about your shitty life."

Finn laughed. Okay, perhaps boosting him up wasn't what she was doing. But he loved her for it anyway. It took the sick coloring from Chad and made him smile. Finn's mom grabbed him around the neck and gave him one of her famous hugs.

"Look at you. You look so good." Mom let him go so he could hug his dad. Dad had a tight hug that you could feel pressing tightly against your ribs. When he let him go, Dad hugged him a second time and then told him he loved him.

"I love you too, Dad." Finn felt his eyes fill with tears. It had been a few months since he'd seen his parents, and it felt wonderful to have them there. Turning to Rachel, he smiled. "Everyone, I'd like for you to meet Rachel Merkel Manning. This is her brother, Chad Merkel."

"My goodness, Rachel, you're as lovely as Finn said you were." Mom hugged her first, followed by Dad. After his aunts were introduced to her, each of them telling her who they were married to, they headed for the car that was there for them. "I went ahead and ordered us a couple of cars to take us home. I wanted to surprise you that we were all coming."

"You did. I only expected about half this many." Mom asked him if he minded. "Not at all. We have plenty of room, as you well know. And if we don't, you can bunk on the plane."

After being seated in the first limo with his parents and Rachel and Chad, they talked about the things that were going on at home. There was always something going on there, and he was glad to know his family was keeping up with the traditions of helping others as they'd always done.

"We, as a family, have our hands in a lot of things at once. Mostly it's charities and the like." Dad told Rachel that they had the money and loved being able to help those in need. "We've worked on rebuilding the schools too. Mostly to make sure our own children were safe going there. Also, the food pantries are stocked, and we provide meals for the elderly."

"My parents used to do that as well. I do a little of it. Not nearly as much as they did, but I work at it. I have a couple of things going on right now that are taking a great deal of my time." Dad asked if it was the restaurant. "It is. Also, Sandra and my brother. I wanted to thank whoever helped with the filing of the paperwork on the house."

"And to get the divorce proceedings going. I knew all along that my wife was a monster. I just didn't know the extent of her evilness." Chad told them he was also sorry to have dragged them into his troubles. "She's been stealing from the restaurant too. I had no idea until Finn told us. Rach had an idea it was going on, but she didn't know for sure until we sat down with your son. He's a good man, and I know he'll take care of my sister."

"You're family now, Chad. Both of you are. And if we can help, we will in any way we can." Dad laughed. "It took some time to find a way for everyone to be able to help you with this. They all wanted to be your hero. You two are the first of what we all hope are many more of the next generation coming to join our group."

"You're all dragons." Dad told Rachel that most of them were, yes. "I know you must be old, but you don't look any older than I do. I'm assuming you can live a long life being a dragon."

"You and your brother will live a very long life as well. You're never going to age. Never get ill or get any kind of debilitating condition." Following Dad's comment, Finn told Rachel he'd meant to talk to her about that. "We want you to be around for a long time. Not just to get to know you, but also to have our family nearby. My parents gave up their lives for us, and we try very hard to make their sacrifice worth every moment that they lost with us."

"Chad and I lost our parents as well. That's what has Sandra so stressed out. She somehow thinks I shouldn't have been a part of their will at all since I was never their biological family." Chad said that she was as far as he was concerned. "You're just being that way because you know you're going to need me when Sandra comes after us."

"That is true." They all laughed when Chad spoke. "My not soon enough to be ex-wife has been causing a bit of trouble for both of us for some time. I had no idea she was— I guess I did know she was bothering Rach, but it never occurred to me that she'd steal from her. I don't know why I didn't see it before now, but I should have." Dad told Chad that sometimes it's hard to think of someone you're close to stealing from you. "That's for sure. I think I didn't want to believe what sort of person she was. I knew she didn't care for me, not really, but to do that to Rach was uncalled for."

"We'll all talk when we get to the house." Mom asked him if he'd made plans for dinner. Telling her not for this many, she smiled at him. "I'll see what I can—"

"I'll cook." Chad nodded even as Rachel started talking about how much she loved to cook. "It won't be any trouble for me to cook for this many people. I understand most of you are large eaters, so I'll have to make sure I get that down, but I would love to cook dinner for all of us. It will help me get to know Finn's kitchen too."

"Have you decided where you will be living?" Rachel shook her head and told Mom that they were still working out the kinks right now. "That's a wonderful way of doing it. Our waiting until we got to know each other a little better gave us, Xavier and I, the ability to have dragons. It was magic that was afforded to all of us, but we were the ones that were able to use it. I'm not saying that you have to wait to have sex or—"

"Mom. We'll work it out. All right?" Mom's face brightened a little, and Dad hugged her to him. "The only thing we're working on at the moment is keeping both Chad and Rachel out of harm's way. While Sandra is in jail at the moment, they really can't hold her for very long. Not until Rachel files charges against her over the theft at Merkel's."

"Carson and your mom have been digging into a couple of other things as well. Once we all sit down together, we can tell you everything. Like I said, everyone wanted to come and meet the newest two members of the family, and to tell you what they were able to find as well as the things they're working on." Dad touched his mind and spoke to him privately. *Trouble is brewing, son. There is speculation that Sandra might have had something to do with the deaths of their parents. Carson is looking into that. Because of the information from their deaths, they're putting together the pieces to the death of her own mother and father. Her parents died in the same manner as Chad and Rachel's parents, Finn. Even without as much training as I have, I think someone should have figured it out.*

Do you know why no one did? For all I know, Rachel might have thought of it too and looked into it. I mean, as I said, we're only just getting to know each other. I know Mom mentioned magic if we waited, but believe it or not, I'm fine with getting to know her first. She's a complete joy to just be around.

Dad said he could see it. Then he told him what had happened to both sets of parents. *So, as you can see, something is wrong when two families who have become related via marriage would decide to die like they did. Not to mention, I don't see how two sets of adults could have up and decided to kill themselves by leaving a car running in a garage to end their lives. Can you? To me, it's just too convenient. According to Carson, they didn't, either of them, leave any kind of note.*

Carson thinks Sandra had something to do with the deaths, or she knows it? You know as well as I do she can make a rock confess to someone tripping over it. Dad laughed a little. *I don't want either of them to be hurt. I know you can understand that, but Chad is a good guy. A little browbeaten right now, but he's a good man. I think he's hurting more for what he's hearing that Sandra did to his sister than whatever she's done to him.*

I think you're right on that. By the way, you should explain to him about the magic that he's gotten. I'm assuming you can feel what he has. Finn looked at his new brother and nodded to his dad. *Yes. Having the ability to dress himself and to bring things to him as he needs them might give him a little heart pounding. I don't know if he knows this or not, but he does have something wrong with his heart now.*

I didn't feel it until just now. I need to get my head in the game here, or I might screw up sometime. As for his heart issues, the magic given to him from me is making him healthier. I think, for now anyway, I'm not going to share his being healed until he learns to settle down and not stress so much. Understand? Dad told him it was hard when you had a new family. Also, he thought it was a good idea for Finn to slow down a little bit. *No kidding. This morning, if not for April, my new assistant, I might well have gone out without shoes on. Too much going on.*

You'll get used to it.

The car stopped in front of his home. He knew his family had seen it when they helped him move in, but today was different. Today he had a mate here, and she was going to cook for them all. Finn didn't know how long it was going to take for him to get used to having all this going on at one time, but he thought it might be fun to learn.

Chapter 5

Rachel inhaled deeply and let it out as slowly as she could without passing out. It wasn't as if she were nervous about cooking tonight—she'd been prepping the meal all day. But she was slightly nervous about the help she had in the kitchen. The faeries, all three or four dozen of them, were ready to do whatever she told them. Mostly she wanted to ask them to leave her alone, but she didn't voice it. Cindi joined her in the kitchen just as she was ready to toss up her hands in defeat.

"Rachel, this is Joey. He's going to be your faerie. I'm sure you were told about having a male faerie to help you out?" Nodding, she looked at the lovely woman. "Good. That's wonderful you know. So let me help you out with this. Just this one time, all right?"

"I'll take whatever you want to help me with. I'm overwhelmed. Actually, I'm more than that. I'm supernova overwhelmed." Cindi just smiled and turned to the faeries, who were hovering—yes, hovering—above the large island in the middle of the kitchen. "What can you do?"

"Watch this." Clapping her hands, she asked Joey to come forward. When he did, he bowed before Cindi, then her. "Joey, what would you do if you had this many people helping you pick a patch of wild blooms? I think you'd be crazy, correct?"

"Yes, my lady. But they only wish to serve the new princesses. She is the first of them, you know." Rachel wasn't sure what he meant, but the little man winked at her. In a surprisingly loud voice, he spoke to her. "My lady Rachel, there are just too many in here for you to have a good enough room to work in. How about I take care of the faeries for you by setting up a time when each of them can come and serve you? This way, you can choose who you wish to work in the house and in the gardens."

"I have gardens?" Joey cleared his throat. "Yes. The gardens. I would really like a large herb garden. I enjoy cooking with fresh herbs and vegetables."

She wasn't sure, but it looked as if the group of faeries vibrated more than they had before. Looking at Cindi, who told her she was doing a great job, Rachel thought of something.

"If I have a list of things I'm going to serve and use to cook with, could some of them help me with that? I mean, I know there are seasons for things like strawberries and some herbs, but as often as I can, I'd like fresh." Joey turned to the group after nodding once to her. "Would it be easier for them to tell me what they have rather than me asking for what I might not be able to get?"

"My lady." A little blue faerie bowed before her as she landed on the side of the bowl on the counter. "We are magical creatures, as I'm sure you've been told. If you wish for us to have fresh things for you year round, it would be our greatest pleasure to make sure we have them. Working for a dragon, or the mate to one is our greatest dream come true. If it would help you, I will take over the running of the gardens for you. It would be my pleasure."

Looking at Cindi when the little blue faerie bowed so low her head was touching the bowl, Cindi gave her a thumbs up. Asking for a name, something she could call her helper, seemed to have been the perfect thing to say. Her name was simply Blue.

"Yes, Blue, you will serve me well. But if you don't mind, don't say you're serving me. None of you. I'd rather we work together as a sort of partnership on things. I want to make sure since you're helping me, you get as much help as I can give you as well." Blue told her they would love a warm place to live in the colder months, as well as a place to grow the things she needed. "A greenhouse. Oh, I have so wanted a greenhouse since I first started cooking. I'll make plans to have one put in."

"We would love to do it for you." Most of the ones in the room came closer to her, vibrating again with anticipation. "It would be wonderful for us to build a lovely greenhouse for you and us to use, my lady."

"That would be marvelous." Before she could say anything more to them and to Blue, all the faeries with the exception of Joey disappeared. Looking at Cindi, she wondered aloud what she'd done. "I didn't hurt their feelings, did I?"

Laughing hard, Cindi told her she didn't, but not to be too surprised by the size of the greenhouse. Rachel asked her if it would be very small like they were. Laughing harder, they were joined by Finn and his dad. Cindi, between bouts of laughter, told them what was so funny.

"Oh my. Oh, my goodness." Finn laughed and told her she needed to be more precise with faeries. "You didn't by chance tell them you only wanted a smallish greenhouse, did you? Or perhaps told them you only wanted to grow small things?"

"I didn't say anything except I had always wanted one. Why?" He pulled her into his arms, a place she was beginning to enjoy being. When he didn't answer, she asked him again.

"It'll be huge. I don't mean like huge for just the two of us and a few faeries, but as huge as perhaps several large landscaping companies huge, with every imaginable thing they can put in it growing." Frowning, she asked him if he was kidding. "No. I'm not. In fact, I'm betting if we were to go into the back yard right now, it'll be about finished. And so full of plants and herbs that stores will be coming to us for their needs."

She thought he was joking. But after one look at Xavier and Cindi, Rachel had a feeling he might well be underselling the size of the greenhouse. Pulling on her sweater, she stepped out onto the back deck to see where the little people might have gone. It didn't take her long to see. The greenhouse was huge, taller than the house by at least two stories. It was beautifully designed in the front, so it looked like a small house. The greenhouse part going out from the entrance was as long as a football field on either side. She didn't know how it was going to work when she only wanted herbs, but she didn't care at the moment. There was a greenhouse in her back yard, and she'd never been so excited.

Blue came to her when she was standing in front of the doorway. "We have fruit for you now, my lady. There are trees at both ends of the building, so we can bring you things whenever you wish." She entered the opening and saw there was more here than it looked like from the outside. "Soon we'll weave some baskets so we might bring you what you wish. A list will be given to you daily on what you can expect in the way of fresh items."

"This is really huge, Blue. What will happen to all the things we're not going to be able to eat? There are only just the two of us in the house right now. Plus, Mildred, the cook." Blue told her all the food would be enjoyed. Whatever wasn't used would be put back into the dirt to give it what it needed as well. "I love that idea. I'd like to see if we can give as much as is left over to other places who might not have this sort of help. Like the nursing homes or daycares."

"What a lovely idea, my lady." She wasn't sure if Blue was humoring her or not, but let it go. "Currently, we are taking fresh fruit into the house for you, as well as there are going to be small herb jars for you to use tonight."

Blue went over all the things they could do for her, and Rachel had a hard time holding onto her excitement. It was like a dream come true for her, having all this and not having to go without when something wasn't in season

Going back into the kitchen, she wasn't surprised to find fresh strawberries and blackberries on the counter. Also, the little pots were there with herbs in them. Rachel started working right away on the rest of the dinner, ready to tackle the world if need be.

By the time they were bringing her green beans as well as green onions, Rachel had set several of the helpers to work on a salad. Several times now, she'd had to ask Cindi if dragons ate this or that, and she'd been just so sweet about telling her things that went with being a dragon's mate.

There wasn't much difference she could see between the two of them. Rachel liked meat a great deal but knew vegetables had to be consumed as well. Reminding herself to ask if someone could tell her what she was, things were being cleaned up behind her as she cooked.

When the pies were put into the oven to bake, dinner was being plated up and taken to the dining room. All the men carried the heavily laden platters to the dining room without a word about it being something a woman should have been doing.

Dinner was served by the faeries. It was lovely the way they seemed to be excited about helping around the house. It did worry her about getting used to such help and the little people deciding they didn't want to do it anymore. But she would take it as she got it and have fun. When everyone's plate was filled, they all thanked her for the meal and dug in.

The bread was something she made for the restaurant every night. Using the magic of one of the little faeries, she'd been able to make enough so it would last the entire meal. Theo told her she didn't need to bother with dressings either, as they could just put what they wanted on their salad when it was put before them. Not sure if it would work for her, Rachel loved it when not only blueberries covered her greens, but the balsamic vinegar dressing was a perfect addition to it.

"I have to admit when I saw this dining room, I wondered why on earth you'd need one this large. Then when you guys started moving around, I had to wonder if it was going to be large enough." Dover told her every room in all their homes was magical. "Really? How does it work? I mean, it sounds nice, but what will it do?"

"This room is larger because the need was there to have it so." She looked around as Dover explained. "If you wish more natural lighting, say some skylights in here to let in the evening sun, then it will happen."

Not only did the room brighten with the new addition of the skylights overhead, but the room enlarged too. Just enough so when Dover and Hadley pushed their chairs back, they didn't touch the walls behind them.

"The living room, where we hang out to watch the games, does the same thing. The television will accommodate us all by being larger than life. The couch will clean itself when popcorn or something is dropped on it. There is, as I said, magic throughout the house." She asked him about the kitchen. It didn't seem to accommodate her. "I'm betting if you think about it, you'll know it did. Like these bowls you are serving us from—did you get them out, or were they just there when you needed them? Was the pan you needed to cook all these potatoes, something you brought here? I doubt very much anyone in this house would have decided you needed a pan large enough to cook so many bowls of fried potatoes."

Rachel thought about it. "You're right. Every time I needed something, a fork, or a potholder, it was right where I looked for it. Sometimes even when I wasn't sure what I needed, it seemed to appear in the right place." Rachel looked at her brother. "You'll need this in your room, brother dear, to clean up after you get home from work. Can you imagine having everything you need right there at your fingertips?"

"I can't. I was just thinking about having to cook for myself too." He laughed. "Most of the time, when I'm in there trying to figure out what I need to make myself dinner, I don't even have any idea what some of the things are called. Like a whisk—or an egg separator. I know for sure Sandra never used anything in there. Cooking for her was ordering out someplace." Chad looked at her and Finn. "I might just stay here for the rest of my life. I never felt this welcome living at home with Sandra."

"I don't have a problem with you moving here on a permanent basis." Rachel looked at Finn, who nodded at her. "Then it's settled. Once this is finished up with Sandra, we'll sell off your home and move you in here. Or you could live in my home. Wouldn't Sandra be pissed off if you did?" They all laughed, but the more she thought about it, the better she liked the idea. "Having you close would be just what I need at the end of a long day."

"What if you get sick of me?" She just smiled at him. They'd be all right, she was sure of it. "I'm going to remind you how you smiled at me when I suggested you'd be sick of me."

"All right. I just want this thing with Sandra finished." Carson said they could finish it with her and Chad. "I think we'd like for you to. It's become a nightmare with her stealing things and telling great lies. The sooner we can get this taken care of, I think, the sooner we can get on with our lives."

~~~

Sandra waited for her turn to talk to the judge. This was just stupid. Here she was trying to get her life in order, and people were getting in her way. When her name was called, finally, Sandra stood up gently. Last night some of the people she'd ended up sharing a cell with had taken exception to something she'd said to them.

"Ms. Smart, it looks like you had yourself a rough night. Is everything all right?" She told him she didn't want chit chat. "All right then. Let's get down to business. I'll read the charges against you, and you'll tell me if you want to proceed with a trial or not."

"Not." He told her she had to wait. "No. I don't think so. I've got shit to do today, and letting you rattle on about stuff that is not my fault will get me out of here later and later. My husband thinks he's going to leave me. Rachel, the woman who managed to wiggle her way into Chad's parents' hearts, has taken everything from us, and I want to go and tell her the way I feel about what is going on."

"You're here on several charges. Charges, as far as I can see, that will not get you out on bail, Ms. Smart. According to the paperwork I have, you were arrested for assaulting an officer. Trespassing and—" She told him it was her business and her home. "No, it says here as well that you own neither piece of property. The house you were living in was in Chad's name, your former husband, until the paperwork was filed to say he sold it to his sister, Mrs.—"

"Why are you calling me Ms. Smart? The name is Sandra Merkel. And Rachel is not his sister. Also, he's not my former anything. When Chad's parents were younger and oh so much stupider, they adopted that girl. This is what I was talking about earlier. She wiggled her way into their hearts, and they left her things in their will. More money and percentages of things, like Merkel's Mark." The judge asked her why Mrs. Manning wiggling into their hearts mattered to her. "Are you even listening to me? They left her more things than they did their biological son. And as I'm married to him, they left her more than they did me."

The bailiff leaned over and said something into the judge's ear. She'd call them out about being rude, but didn't want to get into another long argument with them about their manners. When the man stood back up, the judge looked at her.

"There are several things here I should point out to you. First of all, the paperwork was on my desk when I got to work today. In it was the divorce papers from your husband. The note with it said you were being abusive to him, and the divorce needed to be settled quickly. Spending only these last few minutes with you, I'm glad now that I did indeed fast track this divorce. So, he is your ex-husband. Secondly, you should get your facts straight before you come into my courtroom, Ms. Smart. According to the paperwork I have in front of me now, it states the will was read, and both parties, Chad and Rachel, were present at the time of the reading. Both of them were in agreement with the way things were handled and signed off on it. Neither your name nor that of any spouse was mentioned in the will, so you have nothing to do with those proceedings." Sandra opened her mouth but was cut off by the judge. "And since the issues you have with your ex-husband and sister-in-law have nothing at all to do with this hearing, then I'm going to ask you, how do you plead to the charges before you right now?"

"Don't you see? It has everything to do with the will and Rachel getting more than my husband. I went to the restaurant to tell them not to change the locks. Merkel's Mark is mine." He told her it wasn't, actually. "It is until I say differently. The house is mine too. I lived there with my husband until he sold it to Rachel, probably for nothing, so she could change the locks on the doors there."

"I'm noticing a pattern here with you, Ms. Smart. It looks to me like you're not welcome in either of their lives. Why don't you just call it a day and leave Chad alone?" Sandra asked him if he was serious. "Yes. You've been locked out of not one but two different places in the course of a day. Chad filed for and got a divorce. And this is from your sister-in-law; it's a restraining order for you to stay a hundred yards from her and her brother."

"You have got to be kidding." He said he had no sense of humor at all. "There is no way she is going to get away with this, Your Honor. Rachel is a conniving bitch who should have been left on the doorstep, or wherever my in-laws were stupid enough to get her from. Christ. A restraining order isn't going to be keeping me from what needs to be done. I hope you're aware of that."

"What I am aware of, Ms. Smart, is that if you disregard this order, you're going to find yourself back here in this courtroom facing harsher penalties than you are going to now. You've been notified the order is in place. If you go near her or any of the properties she owns, or that of the— Is Mr. Manning married to her or not?" The bailiff whispered to the judge again, and Sandra rolled her eyes. Fuck this shit.

"Your Honor, just let me go. I have shit I have to do." He told her to watch her language. "I will not. The last time I looked, this was a free country. I'll say fuck fuck fuck if I want to. There is nothing you can do about it."

"Oh, but there is. Officer, please take Ms. Smart back to her cell. When she's figured out I'm in charge, say next week, we'll try this again." The gavel banged down on the desk, and she was pulled away from the line. "Wait."

She knew he'd see reason. This was going to be good. With it being just before noon, she'd have the rest of the day to get ready for reopening the restaurant after having someone to go in and change the locks back to ones she could get a key to.

"Ms. Smart, I'd like you to come to my chambers with me." They didn't uncuff her as she thought they might. Dragged into the room, she noticed Chad, Rachel, and the man from last night. "You're here to bear witness to the wedding of your sister-in-law and Finn Manning. They decided having you here, now, would save them from having to explain to you that they were indeed married every time something came up about it."

"Whatever they do on their own time is no matter to me. Why do I even care if they're married or not?" It was Chad who answered her. "So? Again, what do I care if he's now in partnership with everything she owns? It can't be much. Your parents didn't have anything of value except the little bit of money they left you and the restaurant."

"No, my parents were very wealthy, Sandra. Millionaires, as a matter of fact. Most of which, as you're aware, Rach received. I have a percentage in all of the business. Again, not as large as Rach does, but enough we could have lived a good deal better than we were. I just never saw the point." Sandra tried wrapping her head around millions when it occurred to her what had been done. "I can see by the look on your face that you're plotting again. It doesn't matter now, does it? We're divorced. I've decided, since speaking to my attorney, that you can have the house we shared. Rachel agreed to sign it back over to me so you'd have a place to live. Or sell it, I don't care what you do with it now. It's paid for, as is the furniture. The car, however, is going to be sold off. You'll be responsible for taxes and upkeep of the house, but you now own it."

Good, she thought. Chad was coming to his senses about this. Once she had him at home again, Sandra was going to show him what it was like to piss her off. She looked at Rachel when she laughed.

"What are you laughing about? Did you just hear him? We're millionaires. I might even let you work at Merkel's again after this." Rachel shook her head, and the judge asked if they were ready. "Ready for what?"

"We're getting married." It took less time to marry Rachel and the big man, Mr. Manning, than it did for them to kiss when they were pronounced man and wife. Rachel looked at her when the man pulled away from her. "I'm pressing charges against you, Sandra. For embezzlement of Merkel's Mark. Also for other things missing at the restaurant. The computer, the—"

"Why the fuck did you have to marry him in order to say those things to me? Christ, you just shackled yourself to someone for no reason whatsoever." Rachel told her she married Finn because he was a good man and that they were meant to be together. "Christ. Give me a trash can, I'm about to puke all over the place because that was so sappy. You can't press charges against me because I'm getting Merkel's back from you. My husband just handed it over to me."

"No. I didn't hand anything over to you, Sandra. I said that you could have the house. Nothing more than that. I won't be paying you support. I'm not going to allow you access to my bank accounts. The credit cards you took out in your name, all five of them are your responsibility as well." Chad smiled at her. "You'll have to get yourself a job too. Someplace where you can get paid well in order to pay for the upkeep of your new home."

"Surely, you jest, Chad." He just smiled at her. "Even if you *are* divorced from me—I'm not saying you are, just if—you're still going to pay me a monthly check. I'm not going to allow you to cheat me out of money anymore."

No one said a word to her, and she was fine with the silence. As they shuffled her back out to the courtroom, Sandra felt like she'd won the lottery. A millionaire. She loved the new title. As soon as she was out of there, the first thing she was going to do was sell the home—it was much too small for what she wanted anyway—and buy out Rachel. Her home was the one that should be hers anyway.

She was taken out to the van, sidestepping the courtroom. Sandra was confused when told that she was going back to her cell. No amount of yelling at someone to tell her what was going on would make them stop for a moment to release her. Finally, at the jail, she refused to get out until she had some answers.

"Why am I here?" The officer told her she'd been sent there by the judge. "I'm to be released, not brought back here. I have my house and my money now, and there isn't any reason for me to be locked up. Let me go, and we'll pretend this didn't happen." Sandra put out her hands to have the cuffs taken off.

"No. Either get out on your own or I drag you out. I'm supposed to bring you here." The officer looked at the paperwork in her hands. "It says here you're to spend time back here for cursing and interrupting the judge. Also, there is the matter of you not paying your fines."

"What fines? I wasn't told about any fines. I was told I could go to my home." The officer asked her who had told her she could go home. She had to think on it a moment. "Well, no one. I was told I could have the house and the money due to me when my in-laws were killed. I have things I should be doing. Not hanging around in a jail cell getting me nowhere."

"I guess you'll be getting nowhere then. As far as you getting money? I don't see any mention of it here either. There is a restraining order against you, and nonpayment of fines. Those are about six grand, give or take a few bucks." Sandra asked her why they were so high. "I haven't any idea, ma'am. I'm the officer, not the judge."

Being taken to a different cell didn't go unnoticed. Sandra now had one all of her own, and there was a new jumper as well as different sheets and a blanket on the bed. Screaming for the officer to come back and answer her got her nowhere, either. This was going to be costing the city money if they didn't get their shit together soon.

As she laid on the cot an hour later, Sandra let the day's events roll around in her head. Some of the things that went on she supposed were all right. Like, why did she care if Rachel was married or not? Or why did it matter that she be a witness to it? Whatever their reasons for it, they were lost on her. But there were nagging thoughts she did have to think about.

What did Chad mean when he told her she could have the house? She knew what she'd hoped it meant, but the fact he'd pointed out she would have to find a job bothered her. Even divorced, he'd have to pay her something, she thought.

Why had they lived as paupers for all the time they'd been married? Millions of dollars were right there, according to Chad and Rachel. If they'd made her aware of it right away, she might not have had to steal from the restaurant to have spending money. Which reminded her, she would have to get her stash out of the house before she sold it. Sandra wondered if the house she was going to take from Rachel had a large safe in it as well.

Millions of dollars wasn't a lot, she knew it. Not when it would be split in half. She supposed Chad would make her share with him. It was his parents who had made them wealthy. There had to be a way for her to take more of it, or at least get a larger share of the money. Sandra wondered if there had been any insurance when his parents died. She'd have to have a chunk of that as well.

Sandra had learned a great deal from when her own parents had died. There hadn't been any kind of policies to come to her. There wasn't a home — her mom and dad had rented their place. Nor were there any businesses to sue to collect from a negligent company. Her parents had gotten into a car one night and killed themselves. To this day, she was happy she'd been saved from death. Sandra had been in the back seat, snuggled up in a blanket, while the motor ran carbon monoxide into the taped up windows. If she had to do any part of her life over, Sandra would gladly have killed them herself. Then she wouldn't have had to answer any stupid questions about why they'd done it. She knew why. Everyone in their little town knew it too. She'd embarrassed them somehow.

Spending a month in the hospital had been difficult for her. If there weren't reporters there asking her questions, there were nurses and doctors in her room having her perform all kinds of tests. They'd been fearful she had too much of the poisoning to function well in society. Well, she'd proven them wrong, hadn't she?

As the breakfast trays were being brought around, Sandra

tried to get someone to tell her when she was going home. No one, of course, had an answer for her. If they thought she was staying here until the judge saw her again, they were out of their ever loving minds.

Chapter 6

Finn sat at the table, using it for an office. He had a lot of paperwork to catch up on, and this was the best place he could find to be able to spread out everything. Every time his wedding ring, all shiny and new, flashed in the sunlight from the window, he'd feel himself smile.

"You're looking sappy again." He kissed Rachel when she walked by him. "I'm sorry about yesterday. I should have taken into account the paperwork I needed to sign in order to get things rolling in the correct direction."

"We both have a lot of sticks in the flame right now. I know we're going to have a very long and fulfilling life ahead of us, and having to work on our wedding night is just one more memory we have to talk about when we're old." Rachel asked him if they'd get old. "Yes. I'm older than you by a great deal. My dad is ancient. I believe he's been around for two or three thousand years. My mom is older than me, but not by much. She was in her twenties when she got pregnant with myself and my brothers."

"How old are you?" He smiled at her. "I'm assuming from your look, I'm going to be unhappy with the age. I can take it. Tell me."

"I'm young in comparison. I'll be three hundred on my next birthday. At Christmas time, as a matter of fact. Theo and I were born on the twentieth, and Dover and Hadley the next day." Rachel asked if they were all born in the same year. "Yes. It's freakishly unusual for a dragon to have four eggs at one time. Mom did it, staying in a cave until we were hatched long enough to care for ourselves. Mostly we spent those two years eating a great deal and learning to fly. We, like our father, were born dragons. It wasn't until later we could become humans too."

"You have two brothers who aren't dragons. How did them being with a bunch of dragons happen?" He told her about the adoption of the two of them. "So George was born in a hospital and left behind. Then Milo, who was older by a year, was brought to your family when his parents were killed in an accident. I bet you guys have seen a great deal being around for that long."

"Not really. Dad has seen a lot. He has fought in wars. Worn armor. Flew the skies when there were others like him around. Dad doesn't remember much about his parents, as he was the youngest of all the Mannings. However, he does remember some things. Computers, cars, and traveling through the sky in a plane were just a few of the things he had to deal with when the world was racing to change. By the time I was born, the world was only changing by degrees with technology. Houses are much the same as before I was born. Cars, too, for the most part, but there are more electrical ones. Food sources still come from grocery stores. Things like you see now were about the same when I was born." Rachel asked him another question, and he had to laugh. "Yes, dragons can cry tears of gems. However, what most people don't realize is they are different for each emotion. When a dragon cries, it depends on the reason for the tears as to what they might shed. Like the tears of grief, they become the darkest of diamonds, hard as the stone here, and unbreakable for any human jeweler to be able to cut. The tears of anger are red rubies. The purest of their kind darken with the hatred they were born from. The clearest stones are from the heart—not love, but something akin to the feeling. They're beautiful and the most common. Those stones could be dropped because of a beautiful sunset or the first blooms of spring."

"You named all but one gem, my favorite. There has to be some kind of emerald in this story." He told her he wasn't lying to her. "I know that. I honestly do. It was my poor attempt at a joke. I'm sorry. Do dragons cry emeralds? If so, what are they derived from?"

"They do, as a matter of fact. The emerald is from love. For the dragon that has found his other half, love will make the dragon so happy that tears of joy, emeralds, will be produced. They are planted then, by the dragon and his other half. Once the tree from the gem is sturdy and tall, the dragon will come back to it and give a bit of himself to it. The emeralds of the tree will be inside the fruit." She stared at him. "I have something for you. I know you have a ring, but this one means so much more to me. I'd like for you to wear it."

The emerald was huge. It had been cut in a way that

showed off the flaw in the middle of it. Finn explained to her how the flaw was put there, and why it was now in the shape of a dragon, a red dragon.

"My dad cried this emerald, on the day Theo and I were hatched. Mom wears the one from the day they were wed around her neck. The flaw, the tiny dragon, came about because my mom's tears mingled with his in a way to contaminate it, what it's called when there is a flaw like this." He asked her if she thought it had been contaminated or made more beautiful. Rachel only nodded her head, her own eyes full of tears. "I didn't think so either. Having it mounted for you was a simple thing to do. My dad, in some of his jobs waiting for my mom to come to him, was a jeweler. He did this for me to give to you."

"Oh, Finn, that is the most beautiful story I've ever heard. It means so much more to me than I could express in simple words." She cried more when he slipped it onto her finger. "I came in here to tell you how much I love you. Then you do this. Finn Manning, I love you so very much."

Standing up, Finn pulled her into his arms, kissing her, giving all the passion and love he had in his heart to her. When she pulled her head back from his, he could see he'd bruised her lips. They were swollen a little and pink. Kissing her again, he smiled at her.

"What I wouldn't give to have the house to ourselves right now." He asked her what she meant. "My brother is on his way home. Your parents are flying around. By the way, can you take me —?"

Finn picked her up by putting his shoulder into her belly. Throwing her over his shoulder, he made his way through the house and out the back door. Once they were on the deck, he kissed her again. Finn was in the yard before he allowed her to say a word.

"Don't be afraid of him." Shaking her head, Rachel told him she was excited to see his dragon. "He's warm. He won't burn you, never you. But he will kill another being who tries to mount him. Understand? My dragon will never harm you, not if he can help it. But I can never give a ride to anyone but you. Or any children we might have."

"When you say kill someone, are you telling me they'd be burnt, or they'd be gone?" Finn told her there wouldn't even be dust from their contact with him. "I see. Good to know. Also, I don't know if you're aware of this or not, but I've never been afraid of you. Pissy? Yes. But never have I been afraid of you."

Letting his dragon go was a wonderful feeling whenever he did it. But today, doing this for her, it was something special. He and his dragon had a mate. He wanted to show off for her.

"Oh, Finn. You're beautiful. Or whatever a beautiful dragon can be. You're a great deal bigger than I thought you'd be too." She came off the deck and put her hand out to touch him. "May I? I don't want to startle him into hurting either of us."

You can touch him. He would love it. As soon as her fingers touched his front leg, his dragon purred for her. It was a sound he'd never heard coming from him before. *He loves you too.*

Lying down on the grass, he watched as she walked around him. Keeping himself still, his tail, especially so it wouldn't cut her, Finn loved the fact she didn't seem to be the least bit nervous about being around him. When she made her way to his face again, he stared at her.

"Your eye is bigger than I am. I thought you said you weren't as large as other dragons." He promised her he was smaller. "Then remind me never to look this close up at the rest of your family. I think it would give me a massive stroke."

Would you like a ride? If you call for Joey, he'll make sure you have a safe place to sit while I take you to the skies. Joey was there even before he finished speaking. As the harness was put around him to hold onto the seat Joey had fashioned for her, Finn kept an eye on the things around him. She asked him what he was doing. *I can knock down a tree in seconds. Burn a forest down in less time than you could blink a dozen times.*

"I guess I never thought of the things someone so large would have to take care of. Of course, you've been a dragon longer than I've been alive, which is more than likely why you know to be careful." When she was making her way to his back, she cut her finger on one of the hundreds of scales along his wings. "Damn it. And you told me several times to be careful. I don't want to go in for something to put over it either. Do you think it will be all right?"

Let me lick it closed for you. I can figure out what you are while I'm at it. She nodded and was helped down off the harness. *It's much larger than I thought, Rachel. I'm so very sorry.*

"It wasn't your fault. I'm the one who wasn't being careful getting up there." As soon as his tongue closed the wound, taking her blood into his mouth, he had a moment of uncertainty, a feeling he'd not had in such a long time. "What is it? Do you taste something I don't want to know about? Don't tell me, not until we get back. Unless it's vital you tell me now. Either way, I don't want to know right now. No. When we return is going to be much better."

She didn't mention it again as he took off skyward. Her laughter made him smile and feel wonderful. Even as he did some moves with her back there, never once did she tell him to stop or to not flip again. Nearly an hour later, his parents joined them. It was the first time in a very long time he'd been able to fly with them without the restrictions of other dragons flying into their space.

When his parents left them again, he knew they understood they wanted to be alone. There weren't as many mountains here, not like there were at home, so he flew them to a place he knew would be private. A place the two of them could be alone.

Landing near the small stream where it trickled down from the mountain, he told her where they were. "Are you serious? You flew us all the way here?" He told her he was larger than a car and could travel great distances without much trouble. "But it's so far away. I mean, it seems far to me."

It's not. When she climbed down from his back, he laid down on the grassy area and watched her explore. There was much to see from here. The views were outstanding, and so much nicer than anything he'd ever seen before. *When I was a child, a dragon child, I remember my parents taking us to all sorts of mountain tops. I learned the names of trees. The way the earth interacts with all the things upon it. Even the smallest stone has a function in the way the earth evolves into what you see now. The earth and all its glory is something so few people care about anymore.*

"I guess it's the phone world now. I've noticed you don't even carry your cell around with you unless you're out and about. I think it has a lot to do with the fact that you can mentally speak with most anyone you want to."

You can do it as well. Finn let his dragon go and stayed where he was as his other half. The human side of himself still watched as she leaned in to smell the late blooming flowers and touched the trees, careful where she walked. "I brought you here to make love to you. But I'm enjoying watching you just being yourself."

She turned to him and smiled. He'd never noticed before how much a smile could warm a person's heart. Walking to him, Rachel spoke to him about the things she wanted to do to him. Finn was hard as stone then, and ready for anything she wanted to do to him.

"I'd like to explore every inch of your body. Touch your skin. The thought of your body inside of mine is more than I think I can bear. But I'm willing to give you my all if you are willing to take it." He told her that he loved her. "I love you as well, Finn. It sort of evolved, much like the earth did. My love for you is eternal."

"Come to me, Rachel."

She moved toward him, taking off a bit of clothing with each step she took. By the time she reached him, she was gloriously naked, and the most beautiful creature he'd ever seen.

When she sat down on her knees between his outstretched legs, he reached out to touch her. At her request, however, he put his hands behind him to hold him upright. As soon as she touched her fingers to his lips, Finn knew he was going to be in real trouble. It was all he could do to hold onto his climax until he could be inside of her.

"You're always warm. I can understand, but do you ever cool down?" He told her she was the one making him hot right now. "Ah, I guess I am. I want to make you hotter, but all I can think about is having you make love to me right out here in the open. Would you like it as well?"

"More than anything." Pulling her to him, he was glad

when she put her legs around his hips. "I can take you like this and explore the parts of you calling to me."

"You mean my breasts? Taste them, Finn." He did, taking them both into his mouth at once, suckling at her nipples as she rode his body. "I need to have you inside of me. I want you to make me feel whole. To feel everything."

Kissing her, really devouring all of her mouth, Finn removed his clothing. With the magic that comes with all dragons to shift in and out of clothing, he thought this was the best thing he'd ever used it for.

Picking her up, he held his cock as she lowered herself over him. Christ, Finn thought, she was hotter than he would ever be and cried out the moment she adjusted herself.

"Finn, make love to me. Please?" He rolled her over to her back, never leaving her warmth. "Yes, please. I need to come so badly."

Wanting to make it last, he felt sweat run down the length of his back. Rachel's nails dug deep into his back, and his dragon roared at him to mark her. When she wrapped her ankles around his hips, Finn cried out. It was too much right then. It was just enough to take him over the edge of sanity.

~~~

Rachel had never felt this way about sex before. It really wasn't sex, she realized, but making love. Even discounting that it was outside, they were both needy, and Finn was making love to her in a way she'd never experienced.

Holding him tighter to her, she knew the exact moment when her body was ready to come. It was like everything in her had shut down for just a second too long. When she released, Rachel released every part of her body.

Screaming out, crying loudly so something within her could come as well, Rachel felt lifted up by it. Her body seemed to be renewed, energized, and ready for more. Finn seemed to understand she needed more and doubled his pounding of her. His hands were all over her, just long enough for him to warm her skin then move on. When he cried out that he was coming, Rachel looked at his face and knew there would never be another man who would love her like this. Nor make her feel like she was the most precious person or being in the world.

Coming a second, third, then fourth time, Rachel couldn't breathe. Her heart ached, it was racing so hard. As soon as Finn came again, she knew neither of them would survive this if they did this often. Giggling a little when he collapsed on top of her, she closed her eyes and fell under the spell of darkness. Just for a moment, she told herself.

Opening her eyes when someone said her name, Rachel didn't know where she was at first. Opening her mouth to ask what he was doing, Finn put his hand over her mouth and pointed to her right. Looking at what he'd pointed out for her, Rachel couldn't believe what she was seeing.

"They're new hatchlings. I've never seen them before." Nodding, she watched the three little dragons tumbling and falling all over each other. "They're learning how much strength they have. It's difficult for little dragons to realize they can, even at their current size, knock over a house. These three were born of dragons. You can bet Mom and Dad aren't far away."

"Will they hurt us? Oh, Finn, we're—we're not naked. How did you do that?" He told her about the magic every dragon had once they could shift. He told her she had it as well. But here, with the hatchlings, he had dressed her. "Thank you. But will their parents harm us for being here?"

"If they had a problem with us being here, the hatchlings wouldn't have been able to come this close. I would bet they can smell that I'm a dragon. Also, more than likely that I'm a nephew of the king. Everyone knows of Uncle Cooper. Most even know him." She'd forgotten Cooper was king of all dragons. "Look over there, Rachel. You can just make out their parents hidden in the trees."

It took her a moment to see them. It wasn't until one of them moved, a slight adjustment, she thought, that she knew what to look for. Almost as if they knew they'd been seen, both of them came out of the trees, careful of knocking them over, and bowed before the two of them. Their hatchlings stopped playing and looked to their parents.

"Sit up slowly with me, and they'll come to allow you to touch them now. They won't harm you, not so long as I'm here. And now you have my scent on you, you could be here alone, and the other creatures of the forest and beyond will come out of hiding." She put out her hand and watched as the little ones came toward her. Checking, she noticed to make sure their parents were all right with them moving toward the two of them.

"They're cold. I thought because they were fire breathing, they'd be very warm." One of the small creatures climbed up on her lap, then settled in the crook of her arm. "I think he likes me."

"I would imagine they all will." Soon it was mayhem. All three of them were wrestling to sit on her lap to be held. "They're trying their best not to hurt you, but they're young, so be careful."

It was fun, playing with them and watching them vie for her attention. When a loud clicking noise began, all three of them got off her and Finn and looked in the direction their parents were. Rachel looked as well, holding her breath as one of the large dragons came toward them.

"Finn?" He told her it would be all right. "Christ, she is huge. Much larger than you, and even bigger than I could have imagined. What is it she wants from me?"

"In human speak, his name is John. He's a pureblood dragon, as is his wife. They have been hiding away for decades to keep their children safe." The large male dragon moved close enough to them she could feel his cold breath. "John said you're the first human his children have come in contact with, and he was happy it was with you."

"How do I thank him?" Finn told her she could bow before him. Standing up, she bent to her knees and lowered her head to the ground. "That's not what I meant, but you've pleased him greatly, Rachel. He has a gift for you."

"No. Tell him it was gift enough for me to be able to touch his hatchlings. I loved being able to be their first contact too." Finn laughed. "What did I do now?"

"Nothing. He said you were a very lucky female to have such a kind dragon to keep you safe. I told him I was the lucky one for having your love. Jon said you're the kindest creature he's ever met." She sat up on her knees and looked at the dragon. "Jon said if you speak to him, he will understand you."

"Can he shift into a human?" Finn told her he could not. He was only a dragon. "A magnificent dragon. His mate, too, is the most beautiful creature I've ever seen."

The female came toward the two of them as well. As she laid

her head onto the ground, Rachel stood up to go to her. It was then she noticed her right eye was missing. The scar running across the opening was dark with age. Rachel touched the scar, which was longer than she was tall. She spoke to the dragon.

"I don't know who would do such a thing to such a beautiful creature. I'm sorry to the depth of my heart you were hurt this way. If it was a human who harmed you, I hope his guilt put him into an early grave." The female didn't move, so wrapping her arms around her as best she could, Rachel told her again how sorry she was. "I hope your hatchlings grow up to be as kind and as beautiful as their parents are. Please be safe and love your children more with each passing day."

Hugging her, Rachel felt her eyes fill with tears. She wasn't sure why she was crying, though her heart did hurt a little for what had been done. Moving away from her to wipe at her tears, she looked at the female's mate.

"You're a good dragon, sir, for allowing me to meet your precious family. I've never been more happy than I am for the experience you've allowed me to have." She bowed once again, and he laid his head on top of his mate's. "I don't know what help I could offer you and your family, but if you ever need anything from me, you shall have it if it's within my power to get it for you."

"Rachel, he wants you to take his gift. He also wants you to come here often so he might go home with a lighter heart like the one you have given him and his mate this day." She nodded at Finn when he continued. "The gift being given to you is something he's never bestowed on any living thing in his life. He is giving you the gift of sight."

She waited for more of an explanation, but none came from

Finn. As soon as the two adult dragons stood up, Rachel wanted to beg them to come back to her. The male bent again. This time he didn't lay his head on the ground but turned his massive head, so his sharp horn like appendage was close to her body.

"If you want to accept his gift, you need only to touch the tip of his impale. That is what dragons call part of their armor. It is very sharp, so you need to be extra careful when you touch him." Rachel noticed her fingers were trembling as she moved toward the offered horn. "Gently now."

The touch was as soft as she could make it but still painful. When she was moving her hurt finger to her mouth, the dragon clicked at her. When she stopped, he licked the wound, as well as the rest of her body. Laughingly, she thanked the big dragon.

The dragons left soon after, taking the little dragons with them. As soon as they disappeared into the trees, she realized they were more than likely still standing within the treeline. They blended into the trees and other forest around them because of what they were—dragons who could camouflage themselves. She turned to Finn and asked him if she was right.

"You are, as a matter of fact. Dover is a pearl dragon, the same as they are. As his dragon, he needs only a few seconds to make himself disappear into whatever is around him so no one can find him. I think it's saved his ass a few times over the years." It excited her that she'd figured something out. Then she asked him why Dover was different than his brothers. "We're all different in some way. I'm a red dragon. Theo and Hadley are diamond dragons. It means they can cut through anything with their breath. While they still have fire, the ability to change their breath when needed is what makes them special."

Leaving the mountain top was difficult. She thought she

could have stayed there for the rest of her days. Climbing up onto Finn's back after he changed into his dragon, she was less terrified than before, so she could look at the scenery below and beyond her.

They were flying fast, she realized. While she could see houses and cars below her, the scenery changed with every flap of Finn's massive wings. The snow on the mountain would give way to the lakes and ponds of a city. Larger homes were easy to spot, but smaller ones were just tiny dots on the ground. There wasn't any way for her to look at people. She knew they were down below her, but much too small for her eyes to make out.

Landing where they had started from, their back yard looked boring to her now. There wasn't a dragon lurking in the trees. No babies playing in the soft grass. They did have a lovely and large back yard, but it now seemed to have lost a great deal of its luster. Realizing what she was thinking, she turned to Finn to thank him for such a wonderful day. However, he was staring off in the distance, along the same boring tree line she'd been complaining about. Rachel turned back slowly to see what had Finn looking so tense.

"Rachel, I don't want you to move from this deck. I'm not kidding. Don't take a step off of here until I return." She said she'd stay there, then asked if he would return. "I will. Something is in trouble. I'm not sure what it could be, but it's calling to me for help. I must go."

"Of course. Just be careful." He promised her he would at all cost. "See that you come back to me all in one piece too. Or I'm not going to be happy with whatever is going on."

"I promise."

Kissing her quickly on the mouth, he moved down the

stairs. Before she could begin to think about how he was going to help someone, flames of white hot fire engulfed him. *I'm all right. This is my human battle mode. I'm not hurt, but I can protect myself better.*

"I'll be here when you return." He nodded and moved toward the trees. All she could think about was that he was going to be hurt, and she'd be all alone for the rest of her days.

Chapter 7

Finn saw Shadow before she heard him coming. Letting his fire go, he waited until he was cool enough to approach her. He didn't want to scare her. The little cemetery was something he'd not noticed before. The bench that Shadow was sitting on was older than the marker in front of her.

"I know you're here, sir. I may be grieving, but I am still aware of my surroundings." He moved out from behind the shadows of the woods and approached Shadow. "I found my way to where the home was that I shared with my sisters and our children. It's gone. Even the buildings, stone walls, are now back to the earth we'd dug them from." He told her he was sorry. "As am I. I had hoped at least my daughters' children would be here. Or close by. But they're all dead. All of them have died, with only these stone slabs marking their life. I missed them all."

"Do you know what killed them, Shadow? I can find out if that is your wish. I would very much like to be able to ease your heart from this pain. However, since I cannot take away your pain, I can try and give you comfort in knowing how they died." She told him it might well be terrible too. "Yes, I suppose it might be. I can find out or not, but it's entirely up to you. The dates on this marker, I can only assume it may well be your sister?"

"Yes. It is her. She was brilliant when it came to casting spells. Caroline. We had no last name to speak of, so that is what all who knew her called her. She died so young for a witch of her kind." Finn put his hand on the stone marker and knew just what the woman had died of. "Influenza, wasn't it? She contracted it and died from it."

"Nay. She died in labor. The child also passed in his struggle to be born. I'm so sorry." Shadow nodded at him, knowing he'd not lie to her about something so painfully close to her heart. "There are others here with no last name. Shall I tell you their stories as well?"

"My daughter first. I gave her all I had when I knew I was dying. I should well have lived for decades more, but the humans came to see us for potions and left behind their sickness." Finn asked her what it was she'd died from. "A man, ungrateful for the magic he paid for, came back and cut me nearly in half with his ax. My daughter was well hidden, or he might have gotten her too."

"I'm so very sorry for your losses, Shadow. Let me have a look at your daughter's stone." Finn and Shadow moved between the old markers, looking for the one with the name Serendipity on it. "Here she is. Her marker is nice, don't you think?"

Someone had taken the time to carve the stone into a heart.

On it was simply the name with no other dates like there might well have been today. He touched his fingers to the stone and felt the warmth. It was something he rarely ran into when touching the stones of the dead. Serendipity was well loved.

"She was happy in her years before being settled here after she passed. There were no children of her. Nor did she find a man she could love. While happy with her lot in life, helping others to get well and to live longer, she was lonely. She missed you." Shadow asked who had done such a good job on her marker. "The townspeople paid a man to carve it for her when she passed away. Serendipity was not just a good witch, she was a teacher of adults to help them read and write, including the town's mayor. Your daughter was very old when she passed away in her sleep, Shadow. Hundreds of years old, and well thought of."

Sitting on the ground, Shadow sobbed until he thought her heart was going to break in two. He didn't intrude on her sorrow but watched the surrounding area. Someone could come up on her now, and she'd be in no shape to save herself. It wasn't until his mom and Rachel came out of the trees' darkness that Shadow tried to regain control of her emotions.

"I'm sorry for your loss. I don't know how I would feel to know that my child was gone from this world."

Mom helped Rachel steady Shadow as they moved to the bench again. Rachel stayed with her as his mom came back to him. He could hear them both speaking but didn't interrupt them.

"This is a very lovely cemetery. How did you know it was here?" He said he'd felt the sorrow and worried about who it might be. "I'm glad you came to her aid. Also that you told her the truth of their deaths. It would have been more painful for her had you lied and given her a better story."

"I told her in the way I would like to have been told something terrible like this." Mom wrapped her arm around him, and he put his arm on her shoulder. "Mom, I'm not rushing you, but when are you going back home? There are a few things I'd like for you to do for me before you leave."

"I'll do just about anything for my children, and you know it." Kissing her on the forehead, she smacked him on the chest. "What is it you need to have done?"

"I know who and what Rachel is. I'm just worried how she'll feel when I tell her who her parents are." Mom asked him why. "I don't want to say right now. I have to look up some things on my own to see if anything I think is real or not. I could be wrong, and if I am, what I have to say will hurt a lot of people. I want you to be there for Rachel when I tell her. Not that I couldn't be. But you'll be better at helping her cope with the news than I will. I fear she's going to be hurt badly from this."

"I'll stick around then. When are you planning to tell her?" He told her soon. "I hate that this is going to cause her trouble. She seems to be so happy all the time now. Don't you think?"

"I do. I don't know if it will make her sad or not, but it is going to change things for her. And more than likely, her brother as well." Mom asked him what else he needed for her to do. "Ah, this is a good one. Can you talk to her about dragons? Not just myself and what you know, but all dragons?"

He told his mom about the encounter they'd had today, and the gift the larger dragon had bestowed on her. Finn told his mom he wasn't entirely sure what the gift of sight would be, but it might help Rachel to have a better understanding of dragons in general.

"I would be honored. She's going to be a good addition to the things you have going on here. I hope this thing with her sister-in-law can be settled soon enough. She's in jail still? If you want, I can make sure nothing comes from her again." Mom wiggled her brows and laughed when he did. "No one will ever know I was there."

"How about we use your idea as a secondary plan. I don't want to have to replace an entire jailhouse because my mom got overzealous with her magic." She laughed with him. "Mom, I never in all my life thought I could love another woman as I do you. You were great role models, you and Dad, and I don't think anyone could have taken care of us the way the two of you did."

"That's the nicest thing anyone has ever said to me." She hugged him tightly. "Oh, Finn, whatever am I going to do while you're on this end of the country? I miss all my boys. All of you have grown up much too fast for me."

"I don't think any of us tell you this often enough, but I love you, Mom. With all my heart." He looked over to where Rachel was sitting with Shadow. "I thought for a time Rachel was going to be Shadow's daughter. I haven't any idea why that popped into my head, but once it was there, it sort of kept reminding me to figure this out. For the two of them."

"I'm glad you've done this for her. But I'm really frustrated that you won't let me look." He reminded her that he was a grown man. "Not to me. You and the others will always be my baby boys."

He noticed Rachel stood up and hugged Shadow when

she did the same. They were both visibly upset. When they reached him, Rachel laid her head on his chest. Wrapping his arms around Rachel, he asked Shadow if she was going to be all right.

"Yes. I believe I will." Her smile was the first one he'd seen on the woman. "Your mate is smart. She's offered to help me find a job so I'd not be so lonely. In that, I asked if I may put in a shop for wizards, warlocks, and witches. That's what I'm calling it. I don't know how much need there is for such a shop here. I do think I'll have fun talking about my trade."

"Good for you. You'll be the first person we've been able to help out." He told her what kind of things she could get from the Manning Foundation. "We'll even help you with the purchasing of a building and getting it ready for your opening. It'll help you in ways I don't think you realize."

"I have something for the two of you as well." Before he could ask her what it might be, she touched her hand to his cheek. "You will enjoy the benefits of this until the end of all time."

Staggering back, he was sure he was going to fall right on his ass. However, before he could steady himself, his body started to hum. Then the trembling began. Finn wasn't sure what was going on but knew he had to get down to the ground, or he was going to fall hard. Sitting down, however, didn't make anything better.

"Are you all right?" He looked up, realizing at some point he must have passed out. The sun was definitely lower in the sky than it had been when he'd talked with Shadow. Then he wondered what it was he was given. "Finn, if you don't answer me, I'm going to kick you awake."

"You're just rude, and you know it." Rachel sat down beside him as he lay there. "What did she give me?"

"I don't know, but we both got something. While waiting on you to wake up and tell me you're going to be fine, I did discover this." She put out her hand and snapped her fingers. A blue ball of flame appeared in her hand. "I was thinking about a nice warm bath when I put out my hand. Suddenly there it was. A ball of flame in my hand. I don't know why someone would want this as a superpower, other than a dragon, but there you go."

"See if you can toss it away from you. Like you're throwing a ball." She did it, and the little ball of flame skittered and bounced until it stopped. The fire burned for a moment, only to be snuffed out by a faerie. "I think it would be useful if you were ever in a situation where you need to hit someone."

"Okay, I can see where it could come in handy. What about this?" She stood up and closed her eyes before looking at him again. "Just don't freak out. I don't know if I wouldn't run when I see this, and I know what is going on. I figured it out when I realized my hand didn't blister or even get warm. It was then I discovered I could actually set myself on fire. Ready? And don't touch me."

She closed her eyes again. When she caught fire, no other way to describe it, he felt his heart pound harder than he could hear over it. Standing up, he reached for her, and she told him no.

"I'm a red dragon. I can withstand heat better than anyone." He put his hand on hers and wasn't surprised when the flames engulfed him as well. "We share this. I'm betting we'll be stronger and hotter as a couple. I don't know what we'd need to share our power like this for, but we have it. Where did Shadow go?"

"She went into town with your mother to look at buildings. I didn't do anything wrong, did I? I mean, in telling her we'd help. Well, I said I'd help her, but you added the Manning part." Finn asked her what she meant. "I don't know. Stepping on toes or something along those lines. I have money. A lot, just so you know. While I worked, I did have time to look at stocks and such while the computer was running."

"The foundation has a great deal of money as well. More than enough to give everyone a million dollars, and we'd still be wealthy. I'm not sure if he was right or not, but my dad said that to each of us all the time. Then he'd say, just because we have it doesn't mean we keep it. Helping people is a way to make sure that while you're having a nice dinner, you can feel good knowing someone else is having one too." Rachel told him she liked his answer. "I do too. By the way, my parents both like you a great deal."

"I like them too. I love it when your mom is trying to get answers by skirting around to it. I usually end up embarrassing the shit out of her until she gets frustrated then blurts it out." He laughed with her. "I do have some serious things to ask you, Finn. Are you going to tell me what you've found out about what I am? If so, does it repulse you?"

"Yes, I know what you are, and it isn't repulsive. I think I might even be able to tell who you are. But not right now. I have a few things I need to research yet." She nodded but looked disappointed. "Don't be sad, Rachel. This is a good thing. At least now, you're going to know just what you are. I promise you it's nothing you need to worry about. It's all good. I'm just wanting to put my ducks in a row before I tell you."

"Don't wait too long. I'd hate to have to murder you in your sleep."

He kissed her, loving how she was so loving and violent at the same time. He loved her so much and felt lucky she'd come into his life.

~~~

Pem looked out beyond the bench where she was sitting. The ocean was as pretty as everyone thought it should be, she supposed. Today was a slow day, but still, there were perhaps fifty people walking along the beach. Few were actually in the water—most of them were walking along the water's edge. It was too cold for anyone to be out there for very long. By the time lunch came, there would be wall to wall people. Sighing heavily, Pem stood up to go to her doctor's appointment.

It hadn't been her idea to see a psychiatrist. In fact, she would have been fine with not seeing anyone at all. Pem figured she'd been going to see someone about her mental state since she'd been a child. Now, as an adult, it was ten times worse than before. However, there were better drugs out there.

Her depression would take all sorts of tolls on her, both mentally and physically—sometimes at the same time. She'd not only been unable to work since she'd been home, but she'd also not been able to do much of anything, not even drive a car. These last few months had been utter hell. Even trying to end her life once and for all had been a failure.

Entering the building, Pem ignored the kids in the corner who were playing with the toys. One of the little buggers had snot running down his face onto his lip. When he realized what was going on, he wiped the entire mess on his sweater sleeve.

Pem looked at his mother. Without knowing a thing about her, Pem decided she didn't care for her. Her hair was like all the other women in the room with her, sporting the same haircut. Also, if they were to stand with their backs to her, she'd not be able to pick one out from the other. They were wearing the same stressed jeans and the same short boots with frilly socks out the top. And their cell phones were plastered to their faces.

Snot Nose was looking at her when she turned her gaze from the mothers. While she didn't have a lot of first hand knowledge about kids, Pem figured Snot Nose was about five. She had a niece and a nephew who were about the same age. Thinking about them had her thinking about her brother, Austin, and his typical rich wife.

His wife would have gotten along just fine with the women here. Donna was a joiner. Not a doer, never one of those, but she would join all sorts of committees and clubs only to drop out when it got too trying, stressful, or just plain boring. The one that came to mind when she thought about Donna and her quitting was the women's tea dinner.

Donna had been asked to bring in a dessert to the dinner. That's all. There wasn't even a rule that she had to make it herself. But according to Donna, picking out a cake at the bakery was too stressful for her delicate condition.

Another reason she didn't care for Donna was her inability to use terms so everyone could understand her. Her "delicate condition" could be anything from a headache or to being too busy today getting her hair done at the parlor. Pem thought about her own hair and how messy it was. Tied to the back of her head with an old shoestring, Pem purposely let parts of it hang out of the string just to piss her off more.

"Pembroke Black?" Standing up to follow the nurse, Pem answered her questions as they walked down the hall. "Have you been taking your medication every day? On a scale from one to ten, how would you rate your depression? Any changes in your diet?"

"Yes, I've been taking all my meds. Diet? I'm not on one." Just as she thought, the nurse didn't hear her answers. She just went about her business, taking blood pressure and temperature. As for the one to ten question, the number would be well higher than a ten. "Is my paperwork sent on to my new doctor in Texas?"

"I'll have to check on it for you." Pem nodded, knowing when the nurse left this room, she'd be going on to the next patient and forgetting about her and her request. Pem was told to go back to the waiting room where she'd been called from. "The doctor will be out to get you in a few minutes."

Going back to her seat, Pem sat then lowered her head, avoiding eye contact with the rest of the crazies. There were all manner of people in the waiting room with her this time. Pem wondered if they were in a group setting if they would tell their stories about what brought them to this place. Hers had been court ordered because she'd failed at her attempt to end her life. She thought there was a saying, third time was a charm. It hadn't been. Even after the sixth attempt.

Going into the office to speak to the doctor when he called her name, Pem sat only when she'd been told she could. She, like the people she'd been with when she was hurt, followed orders to the tee.

"What have you been doing these last couple of weeks? Have you been taking your medication every day?" He looked at the paperwork the nurse had given him when she'd brought her into this office. "You've lost eight more pounds since our last meeting. Pem, I don't want to have to put you into the hospital again. Why don't you try and make yourself eat more? Get yourself a malt or have a banana split. You need to be adding more calories."

"Yes, sir." She wouldn't, and she was sure he knew it. "I'm moving back to Texas, today if I can manage it. Has my paperwork been sent to the doctor you recommended?"

"I made sure it was sent on its way personally. I've also taken care to make sure he knew the complete circumstances as to why you were brought here in the first place." Pem wondered what he'd say if she told him he wasn't close to having the entire story. "Ms. Black, why is it you've decided to leave now? You're working at a job you seem to love. You have a nice place to live. It seems…. Well, I'm going to just say it. You know your health issues better than anyone. So I have to think it's dangerous for you to be alone. We're here for you, and we've been there for you when you needed it."

"I have to settle my grandpa's estate."

He looked at her but said nothing. She wasn't one who needed to fill the silence, so she didn't speak. For two entire minutes, he sat there across from her, as if waiting for her to speak. Pem supposed he was waiting for her to explain.

"I didn't know you had any living relatives. What else is it I'm not privy to?" She only stared at him. "Pembroke, I'm disappointed in you. This isn't the way to ensure trust between us. Do you have more things you'd like to share with me?"

"No."

Again he stared at her. Pem wondered if he realized

how much better she was at mind games than he'd ever be. When there didn't seem to be any more to be said about her grandparents, he moved on. Thankfully. The sooner she could get out of this office, the better off she'd be. Closed tight spaces made her ill with the need to be out of doors.

Doctor Shivas talked about the things from their last meeting he felt needed more conversation. Pem was aware he only had part of her medical records. He might know every bullet hole, every burn mark on her body, things that couldn't be hidden away like her emotions were. Pem also knew he didn't have all of the information about her emotional state.

Like, he wouldn't know that while lying on the hospital bed two years ago, she'd assisted in her surgery to remove the bullets from her belly. He wouldn't know that as soon as the surgeon was finished with the operation to remove the bullets, she'd gotten up. The doc had put a towel around her belly with furnace tape to secure it so Pem could operate on a couple more people that were hurting worse than she'd been.

"Are you listening to me, Ms. Black?" She repeated everything he'd been saying. Having a brain like hers meant she could multi-task better than anyone she knew, even if it was talking, listening, and translating all at the same time. Pem could do more than two things at one time. It was what made her job easy on her. "Good. There are some things I think we need to go over before you leave here. When are you leaving again?"

"Today. If I can manage it."

Pem knew she was pissing him off. She could only do what she knew how to do—like her short and curt answers to his questions. Not engaging with people if they didn't start talking first. Also, she didn't want to keep answering questions that had been answered every day this week.

If he wanted answers about things, he should know well enough by now that he had to ask for them. They'd been seeing each other in this building for the last five months. Surely some of the shit she was dealing with would have come out. Like her inability to just lock a door and be done with it.

There were many habits she used to deal with her life. Like the door. The locks had to be checked three times while she counted them. Laundry had gotten easier to do, as she only wore black T-shirts and jeans of the same color. There was a time when she'd have to leave her laundry to when she felt better. Which never really happened often enough.

Before, when she'd had colors in her shirts and different pants, Pem would wash all the shirts of the same color. Even if there was only one shirt of a particular color and nothing else, it was washed all alone. Same with panties and bras. They each had their own time in the washer to get clean.

The silence alerted her that he was finally finished talking. Standing up, he stood as well. Pem knew he had something on his mind, and she was sure she didn't want to hear it. Pem let him speak, knowing he could, of all the doctors she saw here, make it so she'd be in here another month.

"When are you coming back? We won't be in a patient/ doctor relationship then. We could have some dinner, then go back to my house. Unless you would want me to take you out tonight? I'm a barrel of laughs when I'm not in the office." She turned on her heel and reached for the door handle. "Come on, Pembroke. It'll be fun, enjoyable for us both."

He put his hand on her arm, and she stared at it for several seconds before turning to look at him. "Release my arm, or I will hurt you. I'm only going to warn you once. Remove it or lose it. It's up to you."

"You'd hurt me for touching you like this? Christ, you're not going to be in love with the way I have sex with you either." He let her go only to run his fingers up and down her forearm. "We could have a good time, you and I. And for having sex with me, I'll make sure you can drown all your issues in coke if you want it. All the beautiful women who come here resist at first, but after they get their payoff, no one cares what I do to them. Anything you want, I can get for you."

She didn't comment on his statement, even though it disgusted her to no end. Turning her body to the camera she knew was on the wall, Pem knew it also had sound. There wasn't any way she was going to let him get by with this shit while she was here. Pem asked him again to not touch her.

"Come on, Pembroke. You know as well as I do you're not nearly as depressed as you say. I think—and you can agree with me or not on this, but I know that I'm right—I think you're doing this entire dance and pony thing for attention. I mean, after seven tries, you'd think you might have gotten it right one of those times." He smiled at her; his front teeth still had food dangling between them. "I'll even be nice to you for your first time." He touched his hand to her back, and she'd had enough.

Reaching for his hand that was still on her, Pem jerked his arm back, dislocating it. When he screamed, she pulled harder, just enough to make him pass out from the pain. Opening the door, she whistled for someone to come to her. The two nurses and three other doctors came to the room where Shivas was still out cold on the floor. No one moved to check to see if he was all right.

"I warned him twice not to touch me." She told them to call the police. Pem watched as they all stood there looking at their boss. "I'd also like for you to give them the recording of this session with me. I have that right as an injured party."

"Yes, ma'am." The receptionist went to get the recording while one of the other doctors finally got down on the floor to have a look at him, just as she'd commanded him to do. There would be hell to pay on her end, but Pem wasn't taking the chance of someone "losing" the recording of events here today.

"You broke his shoulder." Pem told the other doctor, she thought his name was Tyler, that she'd dislocated it, it wasn't broken. She wasn't sure if it was his first or last name — not that it mattered now. "You know this how? Are you by chance a doctor, Ms. Black?"

Pem told him she was. "I'm retired military USAT — U.S. Army Transport ship. I'm an army surgeon." He asked her if she was joking. "I don't know why you'd think I would make a joke about my credentials, but no, I'm not joking. I dislocated his shoulder because he was taking liberties I never implied I wanted him to do."

When the receptionist came back, she had a CD with her and the phone. She told her the police wanted to talk to her, and for her not to leave until someone got there to do so. Pem didn't take the phone. Phone calls could be edited to have her say anything. It was why she never used the phone if she could at all avoid it.

"I'll go to the cafeteria and wait for them there." No one tried to stop her as she went to the reception desk and put the CD in the computer. Pem found the exact place where she'd entered the room and turned the volume up. The receptionist and the doctor came in while her session was being played out. "I had to make sure you gave me the correct data."

Taking the CD out of the computer, she made her way to the large cafeteria. The smells were of lingering meds, burned milk, and people. Pem was ready to wait in the hallway when she saw they had bottled water as well as fountain drinks. Paying for her two bottles of water, she sat down to wait. Pem had a feeling she'd not be leaving here anytime soon. Waiting wasn't one of the things she did well either.

Chapter 8

Peter sat in the large living room. He'd been asked to come by today by the man of the house. Finn Manning was about the nicest man he'd ever met. For the things he'd done for his pack, Peter would do just about anything. Most of his pack had received their first paycheck since working for the man, and the celebrations had everyone excited for this new adventure. Who knew jobs for a few people could do so much for the entire pack? It was a good sign, he thought, to see his people starting to be more productive at home too.

"Hello, Peter." Standing up, he put out his hand and shook Finn's hand. "I'm glad you were able to come by today. I've been looking into some things, and I wanted to talk to you about them. I also want to warn you that I'm a blunt bastard, so I'm going to get right to the point. Your wife and child, they were taken from you. Correct?"

Peter didn't so much as sit down, but he fell to the couch. An innocent question about his wife and child could do that to him like nothing else could. While he didn't think Finn was being a bastard, he felt his anger surging upward.

"Why are you bringing this up now? Did you mean to blackmail me? I don't know if you know this or not, but I have nothing to top what you have already said. The only thing that keeps me going is the fact that they still might be out there." Finn nodded. "If this is why you brought me here, I think I've answered—"

"Rachel. Would you come in here please?" Peter didn't bother looking at the dragon's mate. He wanted to leave. Finn calling his wife in for any reason didn't matter to him. "Peter. I want you to look at my wife, please."

"Why? What sort of games are you playing?" He glanced at the woman in the room, then looked at Finn. "So what. I've looked and—"

Peter looked again. She was strikingly beautiful. Standing up, he walked as close to her as he could, simply because he was sure he was hallucinating. She was a ghost from his past. Lifting his hand to touch her, careful of moving too quickly and she'd disappear, he was as afraid as he'd ever been. It was the eyes. The eyes of his wife staring back at him.

"I know the papers were saying they thought they'd both been killed and not found as yet. I don't think your daughter is anywhere, but right here." Peter couldn't get over the fact of how much she looked like his own Dalia. "I'm assuming you believe she's your daughter as well. I'm sorry about this."

Peter told his friend not to worry about it. Then he looked at Rachel again. "You look like your mother. So much so, I thought for sure you were her." When she smiled at him, Peter put his hand over his mouth to keep himself from babbling. He wasn't aware he'd been crying until the young lady touched her fingers to his cheek. She was right here, his little girl with the brown curls, the pink cheeks, and freckles. Someone he never dreamed of seeing again. "Do you know who I am to you?"

"Yes. You're my dad. Finn explained it to me last night. I saw that we resembled one another when I saw the picture in the paper about how my mom and I came up missing." Peter asked her if his mom knew it yet. "No. I had to think about if I'd seen her, and I've not. Mildred is off when I go to the kitchen to cook for us. We've been so busy, I've not been able to even go in and chat with her. We didn't want her to know before you if I might be your daughter. I'm so glad to have found you."

"My little girl. Oh, honey, you're my little girl." He pulled Rachel into his arms and held her tightly, fearful, he thought, that she might disappear again, and he knew his heart would never recover from the loss of her a second time. He could smell it now, the wolf she was. "You even smell like her. Her name was Dalia. Dalia Duncan."

"I didn't know I was a wolf. I knew I wasn't wholly human — my adoptive parents had me tested when I was about five. They didn't tell me anything other than I wasn't human. I don't think they cared all that much so long as I was able to fill a void in their lives. I've spoken to the faeries. They said because I've not been around wolf shifters, or anything else for that matter, my wolf lay dormant." Peter told her it was the way things would have worked. He finally let her go but took her hand into his again as they sat on the couch. "Finn found some other information too. Are you ready to hear it, Pop?"

Pop. He was her Pop. Never had anyone called him Pop. Peter had never found himself someone to love after his first and only true love had been taken from him. Now here he sat with his only child calling him Pop. Nodding, he looked at Finn.

"I did a great deal of research on this before I approached you. I'm afraid your wife is dead, Peter. From what I've been able to gather, she was killed almost as soon as she was taken. It was, I believe, a case of kidnapping the wrong woman." Peter asked if it was another pack member. "Yes. The woman they were taking should have been the wife of your brother. He owed, and still does, a great deal of money to some savvy loan sharks. I can fill you in on the rest later if you'd like. Or now if you have the time." He told him now would be good. "All right. The men were hired to take Robert's wife, to hold her until he came up with the money to pay back the substantial loan he'd taken out to gamble. Or to pay down on some of what he owed. I'm not entirely sure which, but it doesn't matter."

"He told me he didn't gamble anymore. Once I bailed him out, he promised he was finished with it for good." Finn asked him how long ago it had been. "Let me think a minute. I think it was about five years ago. It cost me a great deal to help him out."

"Yes, I saw where he'd paid off some of the places he owed money to." Peter asked him what he meant by *some* of the money. "After you paid out the half million of his debts, he was still looking at several hundred thousand dollars he still owed. And he's still gambling and racking up debt."

"Christ. I had no idea it was that bad. I cashed in my insurance money for him. I hadn't wanted to touch the money from the claim on Dalia's death, but after several years went by, I was told as far as the insurance company was concerned, it had been long enough. I don't know how I would have paid it off without the insurance money. The check was just laying on my dresser until he came to me for a loan. Of course, I've never seen a dime of payback since then." Peter looked at Rachel again. Peter thought of something he wanted to tell his little girl. "Your name was Priscilla. It was my grandma's name when she was alive."

Peter couldn't stop touching her skin. He really was afraid she'd disappear. All three of them stood up when the crash of broken plates sounded. Peter's mom was standing there. She was staring at Rachel the way he had when he'd first seen her.

"It's Prissy." Rachel laughed. She then asked his mom if that was what she'd called her. "You're my Prissy. I called you that because you were so beautiful, even as an infant. Peter, please tell me that this woman is— I just realized that you're the lady of the house. Oh my goodness, you're here. Prissy, come hug me."

Mom held onto Rachel tightly, babbling in much the same way he had. There was no doubt in his mind Rachel was his long lost daughter. But to see her with his mom brought on more tears and the need to take her home with him to protect her.

"You're a very lucky man, Peter." He nodded, then turned and asked Finn why he'd said that. "You've been searching for Rachel and your wife for so long, and it was here where you found her. Will you allow me to tell you about your wife?"

"She's dead, you said. Was it a quick death? I want to know if she had to suffer, but I don't at the same time. She did, didn't she?" Finn nodded at him. Rather than look at Finn, knowing something about his family that he didn't, Peter looked at his mom and daughter before speaking again. "Robert didn't like

Dalia. Nor was she very impressed with him. I believe it had to do with the fact she was so strong. As an alpha bitch, she had to be. She made him work and never put up with his bullshit. That was all he ever was, a person who slung shit every time he opened his mouth. But it went beyond them not liking one another in the last few days Dalia was with me. The two of them couldn't be in the same room without a flare of tempers. I don't know why I feel this in my very soul, but I believe Robert might have told them where to find my wife instead of his."

"You're right, Peter. He did." Peter closed his eyes when the pain in his heart was too much for him to bear alone. "The men who took her were told what she drove and a schedule that she followed. Like going to the grocery store on Tuesdays. The description given to the men who came after Robert's wife was of your wife. He'd even gone so far as to tell them what sort of car your wife drove, including the license plate number. She had a price on her head the moment Robert got in over his head."

"How do you know this? Did you talk to those responsible?" Finn told him about one of the things he could do. "You only need to touch a gravestone of the deceased to get the information? That is seriously messed up, Finn. I mean, even as a dragon, knowing you can do something like this is really weird." Peter was trying to make light of the power the other man had but knew he'd failed terribly.

"It comes in handy at times. But I don't have to touch just the grave markers. I can get the information from anything that was touched by a person. Dead or alive. Human or not. While I can't talk to the dead, I can gather fragmented information, or from your wife's grave everything she had happen to her in her final hours." Peter asked if he could make sure the police knew where she was buried. "My aunt is taking care of it for you now. I hope you don't mind, but I told Aunt Carson you'd want your wife buried here. In the cemetery on your land."

"Yes, I'd like her close." He leaned back on the couch when his mom and Rachel came to sit with him. "I've no idea what to do now. I feel like I've been given the greatest gift of all — Holy shit, I have a son-in-law that is a dragon."

They all laughed, and Peter felt like a bit of the tension was gone. There was so much he wanted to hear from Rachel. Also things he'd rather not know. Mom was talking about when Rachel was a baby, telling her things he'd forgotten about in his grief. Peter looked over at Finn and realized this man was much better than he could have ever hoped for in a son-in-law. He was a man of worth, intelligence, as well as honor. Peter thought he couldn't have picked a better mate for his only child.

"Where are they? The men who killed my wife and tore apart my life?" Finn told him they were being taken care of. "That isn't what I asked you, Finn. Where are the men Robert hired to kill my wife and take my daughter from me? I need to know."

"All right. I can understand where you're coming from. The man who took your wife and child was named Manchester. He was killed not long after it came to light they'd gotten the wrong woman. His boss, a man by the name of Whitfield, was the one who pulled the trigger on him. Then Whitfield was killed a week later when another boss came in and took over his network. The other two men aren't dead but are in prison on unrelated charges. Aunt Carson is going to make sure more time is added to their crimes as soon as your wife's body is discovered." Peter thought Finn knew where Dalia was buried. "I do. However, I can't tell people where I found her without raising more questions than I can answer. The issue is that someone wouldn't be able to just stumble over her grave. My aunt is working on someone finding her today."

"I don't understand. Why can't you get involved? Is it because you're afraid someone will think you killed her? I didn't even know you when she was killed." He could feel his anger getting the best of him, and stopped speaking for a moment. "Tell me why you can't just tell me where she is."

"Her body was buried under what is now a garage. The house was already there, but the garage is a new addition. As in, it's being finished up today. Aunt Carson is going to have an inspector go by and say the foundation isn't thick enough. He'll tell the homeowners it must be redone." Peter asked if they could afford the repairs. "Yes, they can now. Yesterday they won a good deal of money from a lottery. It will not only be enough to redo the garage, but they will also get the reward money from the insurance company. They'll honor the reward because Aunt Carson said they would."

"She has pull then?" Finn only nodded. While he thought there was more to the answer than he gave him, Peter let it go. "I can't thank you enough for what you've done for me. For my mom as well. I knew in my head both had been killed a long time ago, but my heart would rebel at even the thought of them being gone from us. However, to have Rachel here, now, it's like I've been given a second chance on life."

"You have been. I want you to know something, Peter. I won't hurt her. Ever. None of my family will. We'll protect her with our lives." Peter said he knew that too. "She is the love of my life. Besides, I think she'd hurt me if I even tried to cause her any harm."

"My mother would hurt you, too, I think." Everyone laughed, which was what he needed. The tension was thick in the room, and Peter wasn't sure why. Then it occurred to him. "Robert doesn't know. He has no idea Rachel is here with you, does he? Does anyone in your family have a plan I need to be aware of?"

"He's going to be arrested as soon as he gets here. Not as soon, but soon after. The house is under the protection of the people my mom and others work for. Mom talked with Rachel last night after I told her what I'd discovered. Neither one of us wanted to have you hurt over this. Mom thought Robert would have less knowledge of my home and wouldn't be able to escape." Peter asked if they thought he'd run. "Yes. He's totally responsible for several deaths. Mom also wanted me to let you know there will be no report on him being arrested and taken in. Not if you want to take care of him your way."

"You'd allow me to have my pack take care of him?" Finn told him it was only fair his pack did it since his alpha had been killed. "They'll likely kill him anyway. I doubt a cell could stop them from getting revenge for my wife."

"As they should have been able to do long ago." Peter didn't know what to say to his statement. Finn was going to let him take care Robert was punished by their laws for what he'd done. "No one, not anyone, will suffer for what you have to do, Peter. As I said, it should have happened long ago. It will be your call."

"I'll take him." Finn nodded, and the front doorbell rang simultaneously. "Is it going to be him?"

"It is."

Rachel and his mom left the room. He didn't know the plan, but when Cindi and Xavier sat down on the other chairs in the room, he didn't know what to think. Robert was shown to the room they were all sitting in. Finn asked him how he was doing.

"Just fine, really. I'm a man who takes pleasure in a lot of things others might miss." No one laughed at his comment. "I didn't know you were going to be here, Peter. I guess I thought I was going to have a meeting with Mr. Manning here. Something about a project. Did he fill you in on it already?"

"No." Peter looked at Finn. When he waved his hand, as if telling him it was his show, Peter stood up to face his brother. "You had my wife and daughter killed, didn't you?"

The look on his brother's face told it all. Peter didn't get angry. He didn't feel the need to face his brother with intent to kill him just yet. He did, however, wonder what had been going through Robert's head when he ordered the death of two people.

~~~

Robert stared at his brother, wondering who might have squealed on him. It could have been any number of people he'd had with him the day he'd signed the contract on Dalia's life. However, he thought most of those people were in jail or dead. He himself had killed off Manchester just a few days after he'd killed Dalia.

"I haven't the slightest idea what you're talking about. I thought she ran off or something." He felt his knees shake a little when Peter's wolf rolled over his skin. "What's really going on, Peter? You look ready to attack me. This isn't the way brothers behave to each other."

"You're going to try and guilt me out of getting answers from you? I fucking trusted you. You had my wife killed so you could get out of some gambling debts, didn't you?" Robert was afraid at how much he really knew about the death of his wife and daughter. "Oh, you can bet what I don't know now, you're going to tell me about it. You fucking bastard."

Robert was told to sit down. From the state of anger coming from his brother, the compulsion to sit made him sit right where he was standing. The floor wasn't forgiving, nor was it very warm. Not moving at all for fear of drawing attention to himself again, he watched his brother be every bit of the pack leader he was.

"Thomson is going to pick up Marie and bring her here as well. I'm going to question you both on your involvement in my wife's death. You should understand something, Robert. The two of you are going to die tonight. I'll give no mercy to either of you. Killing your alpha bitch was bad enough, but you also planned it so that both my daughter and wife were taken from me."

Robert started to tell him again he had no idea what he was talking about, but stopped. Trying to think past his fear, Robert did wonder if Peter would be able to kill him. The written law was very specific, and there were no loopholes in it. It stated that an alpha could not kill or maim his blood relatives or his mate's family for any reason. It was going to be his trump. His get out of jail card for both him and Marie.

"Why did you do this to me?" He'd not realized everyone had left the room except for the two of them. Nor had he noticed when Peter turned a chair toward him and sat down. "Answer me, damn it."

Again, the compulsion. Peter was a good deal stronger than Robert might have admittedly known about. The power to make Robert speak and tell all finally exhausted him in trying to fight it. He looked up at his brother.

"What was I supposed to do? Let her rule me around like I was nothing more than anyone else in the pack? I'm your brother, Peter. We should never have let her get between us like she did. You had to see what she was doing." Peter told him it was her job to order him around. "You allowed her to do this to me? You wanted her to treat me with no more respect than she did any of the others here? Christ, Peter. Even you would have been pissy about having to listen to her harp about me getting a job. I had to help out around the house. I needed to stop gambling. All those things would spew from her mouth every time she was around me. I got sick of it."

"You killed her or had her killed because you're a lazy fuck." Robert might not have put it just like Peter said, but really, he was a lazy fuck. "But that wasn't all you did, was it, Robert? You took my daughter from me as well. Where is she? Do you even care what happened to her? Have you given one thought as to whether she too might be dead out there?"

"One of the men said they'd sell her off. If it's any consolation for you, I did tell him to sell her to a good caring couple. He didn't share the proceeds with me, so I haven't any idea how much he was able to sell her for." Peter just stared at him. "Peter, you know you can't kill us, don't you? It's in the by-laws."

"You have the nerve to quote by-laws to me, you fucking bastard. I should just kill you where you sit. At least then I'd get some sleep at night." He yelled for someone named Rachel. Robert's back was to the doorway, so he could only hear her speak. "Could you do me a favor and ask Finn if he'd go with me to pack land? I need to have him do something for me."

"Yes, sure."

He didn't hear her leave the area, but when his brother laughed, it was all he could do to turn enough to look at what he thought was so funny.

"Hello, Uncle Robert. Do you remember me?"

Robert looked at the woman. When it occurred to him who she was, he knew he was so fucked right now. It was Dalia. She wasn't dead? Not possible. Robert had seen Manchester blow a hole in her fucking head. Rachel, if this was her, leaned in closer to him, just bending at the waist to look him in the eye. Her face was beautiful, just as he remembered. When she put her hand around his throat, the long nails of the wolf she was cut into his flesh. Robert felt his bladder let go.

"So you do know who I am, don't you, uncle dear? Your long lost niece that you let someone sell off instead of manning the fuck up and rescuing me." Robert told her it wasn't his fault. "You have to tell me how you came up with an answer like this one. Did you not owe a great deal of money to Mr. Manchester? From gambling, I heard. You not only supplied him with my mother's plate number and a description of her car, but you even handed him a picture of her so he'd get the right person. How is it not your fault when you simply handed him everything he needed to kill her?"

"I didn't want my wife to be dead. I had an idea he wasn't planning on killing her anyway." Rachel told him he was a liar. "Okay, so I knew what he was up to. Like I said, I didn't want

Marie killed. Besides, your mother was a fucking cunt."

Robert felt two of his ribs break when she kicked him in the side. This shouldn't be happening. She was related to him by blood, damn it. When she got down on her knees in front of him again, he told her the law like he had his brother.

"Ah, but don't you see? When you had me sold off—and I know it was you who sold me to the Merkels, not one of the other men as you claimed—I was no longer related to you. I found the small loophole when I read the by-laws as well." Robert didn't know that. But then, he and Peter were related, so he just figured Peter's daughter would forever be his niece. "You have a sick fucking mind. Did you know? You make me sick."

Marie came in the back of the house, and Peter told him to shut his mouth. He could no more open it to warn his wife than he could have screamed out her name. She was chatting it up with Thomson and seemed to be excited about being invited to the big house. Marie was telling how she'd dreamed of living in this house for a long time.

As soon as she came into the living room, she was told to sit like he'd been told. Marie kept staring at the younger woman until she spoke softly to him. The idiot had to know each and every one of them could hear her.

"I thought you said she was dead. Isn't that what you told me?" He told her to shut up. "I will not. I want to know why I was dragged from my home and brought here. What is going on?"

"I'm what's going on." Peter had never looked so good. In the last few minutes, it seemed to Robert that his brother had gotten taller, more confident, and his muscles were bulging from under the sweatshirt he had on. "You now have the opportunity to tell your side of the story as to why you had my wife killed and my daughter taken from me. I want details. Names and anything else you have inside that fucking sick head of yours. You will both tell me the truth now."

"Peter, we didn't do anything wrong, you know." Peter just looked at him. "My wife means so much to me. Everything. So you can understand why I didn't want her to die. You had your daughter—well, you should have had your daughter to keep you company all the time. I never thought of everything when I sold her to the Merkels. Maybe had you looked a little harder yourself, you could have had her here all the time."

"So, this is my fault? Because I didn't look at every crib in this town, on the off chance you sold my little girl to a family? You're unbelievable, Robert. I can't believe I protected you so many times as the leader of our pack." Peter walked behind him to where Marie was, her back to his, which made it so Robert wasn't able to see her or warn her of Peter's anger. "What did you do when you found out Robert had killed my wife and sold my child? What was your part in all this?"

"What did you expect to happen, Peter? You never took our side in anything she said about us. Every day I was being dragged to the packhouse to go over some minor issues Dalia had with what I was doing. It was difficult enough for us to have enough money to gamble with, without your wife telling us to get a job and help out with the pack." Marie laughed then. It was harsh and something Robert was afraid of when she did it to him. "Your wife wasn't as saintly as you think she was. Did you know it was her plan to send your daughter away to a boarding school when she was old enough? I bet she didn't tell you she was pregnant either. I wonder who it might have been by."

"Dalia was pregnant when you had her killed?"

Robert knew Marie was going to gloat over this new information. He wanted to tell her to shut her fucking mouth. As soon as he felt her back slump against his, he knew his lovely wife was dead.

Robert sat there, his back being soaked by the blood of the only woman he'd ever loved. His own mother was never as close to him in love as Marie had been. Her body was moved, and he fell to the floor on his back. He watched as someone carried her out the back way of the house.

"Get up." Robert stood up but didn't have the strength in his legs he needed to walk. He knew his brother could see he was hurting and did nothing to see to his needs. She was dead. His mate, his wife, was dead. Robert demanded to be told who had killed her. "You lost all rights to demand anything of me when you murdered my wife and unborn child. But I'll gladly tell you who got to kill her before I did. It was my daughter. Slicing her head off her body without a second thought. What do you think of my daughter now, Robert? Want to try and sell her off again? I might watch you trying to convince her to get into the car of a stranger."

Robert fell twice and stumbled several times as he was literally dragged from the house to the yard and beyond. His lip was bloodied—he could taste the copperiness of it. After what seemed like hours, he was in the field the pack owned. Robert got down on his knees to beg mercy from his brother.

"Shut up." He did, his mouth closing off like he'd been born without a mouth. Begging still with just his hands and eyes, Robert pleaded with him to not let him die. "By order of the pack, the Duncan Pack, I hereby sentence Robert Duncan, brother to me, to death. The reasons for it are as bad as they could be for his crimes against my family. He had my wife and our unborn child murdered for money. Then he sold off my only living child for the same thing. Greed and money. I hereby order his death by fire."

Robert thought they were going to set him on fire in the pit they used when here. But as soon as he turned to see how it was going to be done, he saw a big fucking dragon standing right behind him. Screaming now, compulsion having been taken away, he knew he was to die, and watched in horror as the dragon drew in a deep breath and then spewed it all over him.

His last thoughts were that he should have been more careful not to be caught.

Chapter 9

Finn found Rachel on the deck. She'd been missing for about an hour when Mildred came to tell him. Missing wasn't the word she'd used. She told him Rachel seemed to be grieving. Going out onto the deck where she was, he moved to her side, and Rachel looked up at him.

"Did you go there and help them with the death of Robert? I don't care one way or the other if you did. I just wanted to know." Finn sat beside her and took her hand into his. "You're stalling. I don't want you to be unable to come to me when you're trying to protect me."

"Yes, I helped in the death of Robert Duncan. His wife has been killed, as you well know. They had no children, or I would have helped them out. Not for the parents, but because they would be innocent, as well as being family. Marie knew about the plans to have your mom killed as well." Rachel asked him what *he* would have done with the wife. "I don't know. I really don't. I want to say I'd be compassionate about her situation. I want to say she had very little to do with the deaths. However, she knew. And could have—no, she should have gone to someone to tell of the events."

"I agree with you on telling someone about what he did. I don't know, for the life of me, how they managed to be here all this time and not tell someone about it. Or at least let it slip. He had my mom murdered, which is bad enough. But to kill off the tiny life she was carrying was horrific. He had no cares at all about what happened to his only niece and the yet to be born child. It's hard for me to let it settle in my head." Finn picked her up from the chair she was on and held her on his lap. "I have nothing of a memory of my mom. I don't have anything to see of her likeness except for the newspaper article. I know I look like her, but nothing more."

"I asked if there were any items belonging to your mom you could look at. Peter said he'd bring over some of her things for you to have. Also, he would very much like for you to come to see him as much as you can. He's going to be with you when you shift." Rachel said she didn't think she was ready for shifting yet. "I understand. Would you like to come in for some lunch? Mildred said you skipped it."

"Not just yet. I've been thinking very hard on what the outcome has been from Robert killing my mom. Not just her being dead, but other things happening because of her being killed." He asked her what she'd thought of. "Foremost is that I was adopted and not with my own family. I did wonder for a moment if he would have had me killed as well, but I don't think it was his plan at all. Also, from what Mildred said—she asked me to call her Grandma—Peter grieving so hard is why the pack is doing so poorly. Then there are the things trickling down because of Peter being unable to deal with the pack and his missing mate too. There's more, but I think you can understand where I'm going with this. Right?"

"You're saying Robert's death wasn't nearly enough for all the things he'd done in order to get rid of someone." Rachel told him he was brilliant. "I get that a lot."

Rachel smacked him on the chest and laughed. "I was thinking of something I could do to help the pack out. I'm a member of it now, did Peter tell you?" Finn told her Peter had said she was his next in line to lead the pack when he retired. "I'm not ready for anything even close to taking over a pack. But he did tell me he'd train me in being a wolf. To think, all this time, I was so close to my biological father and had no idea. It's sort of sad, don't you think?"

"It is. Very much so. What surprised me the most about it was the number of articles being run about the disappearance of your mom and you. No one in the pack could see how much you looked like her? I guess I find it hard to believe." She told him how she wasn't photographed much when someone would come to their place of business. "Okay, I guess I can see where it is you're coming from. And even if your name was mentioned, without a picture, it would have been hard."

"Exactly. Oh, before I forget to tell you. Chad went by the police station earlier and was told Sandra will be released at two today. They can't hold her any longer than three days. She'll have a fine to pay, as well as face some restrictions. She can't come within a hundred yards of either myself or Chad. She'll violate her restrictions as soon as she's released, I think." Finn thought so too. "Chad has already signed all the paperwork on the house and had it filed to establish it now belongs to Sandra.

He asked me if there was anything in the house I wanted. I told him there wasn't. So he's donating all the household stuff to the halfway house just outside of town if Sandra decides she doesn't want it. I think he put it in the paperwork when he put her name on the deed. It's for female prisoners who have been released. It helps with some of the things missed while in lock up."

"I had no idea. How long have they been around?" Rachel told him at least four or five years. Then she told him where it was located. "The old elementary school? I would guess it's as good a place as any to help women out. There would be a lot of rooms to use."

"Yes. But all the classrooms have been converted to dorm-like settings. When I was there at the grand opening, I was told, along with the other people there, that there would be eight beds in each room. I don't know, but it sounds very crowded to me." Finn thought about how they could use something newer to use. "What are you thinking right now?"

"About how the Manning Foundation could help them out. As you observed, there has to be issues with overcrowding. Not to mention, if I remember correctly, the building was built in the early part of the last century. It has to be getting to the point of falling down around their ears. Wouldn't you think?" She nodded. "I think we can help them out with not just a better living arrangement for the women, but other things they're dealing with too."

"What other things?" Finn explained about the kitchen. "How do you know all this about the building? I mean, I only just told you about what it was being used for. Do you secretly go out at night and hunt down elementary schools for fun?"

"No." He laughed. "When we first moved here, my brothers and I were given paperwork on all the buildings in use. It didn't tell us what was being done in the building, only the specs on it." She asked him why he needed it. "To see where we could start helping the people who are already making a living in the town. It would have told us not only how old the building was, but also if things like the furnace were too old. If windows needed to be replaced. Among other things, we were told how many bathrooms were in the building per how many people lived and worked there. In this case, it would have told us the building has such and such number of people there, and the ratio to how many bathrooms there are."

"Okay, I get it. But what can you do for them? I've noticed government run places are difficult to donate to. Well, difficult is an understatement. It's more like you can't help them." Finn told her it was a private company. "Well, aren't you just full of information today. Okay, smart ass, how do you help them without pissing them off because you know things about their building?"

"I'll talk to my brother, Milo, and have him talk to them. He's good at convincing people of things they might not have realized they needed." Rachel stood up and paced the length of the deck. He loved watching her work things out on her own. "Now, you tell me what you're thinking about."

"You may recall that I have money. I have no idea what your net worth is, but I'm figuring it's considerably more than mine is." Finn told her how much they were worth. "Christ. Are you serious?"

"I never joke about love or money. So yes, we're billionaires several times over." He asked her again what she had in mind.

"I have to think a moment. You have several billion dollars?"

"Yes. What is it you want to do? And so you know, it's us that has money, not just me. We share all of anything I had before meeting you." She told him she had several million, but not a billion. "Again, yes, you do have billions. If you want to use the money you had before for anything you wish, I have no problem with your decisions.

Rachel took up pacing again. Finn knew she'd not tell him anything until she had it worked out. While he was waiting, he contacted Milo to tell him what he had in mind.

You're not going to believe this, but I have a letter from them. They contacted our headquarters a few days ago about needing help with the furnace and air conditioners. There is one in each of the eighteen rooms being used as housing. Finn asked him if he knew what it was being used for. *I didn't before, but I do now. They house women in the place who need to acclimate themselves to the outside world after prison. It's a good cause, I think. They're not funded by anything but donations either. There was a foundation helping for a lot of years. However, the money ran out about the time things in the building started to break down. It says here if we can help them with the installation of a few more bathrooms, it would be greatly appreciated. What is it you have in mind?*

Not helping them with the building, first of all. They're only going to be pouring more money into the building until one day there's just going to be too much work needed. Milo said he thought it was happening now. *I agree. As a not for profit foundation too, I was thinking we need to get them into something bigger and in better shape.*

Finn asked his brother to hang on a moment, Rachel had an idea. "Can the faeries be trusted to build the building they'll need and not go overboard?" Finn told her they had to be shown what was needed. "Okay. But it will have to be built on the outskirts of town. I think I read someplace about boundaries not being close to schools. Since there is one at each end of this town, we have to build out. Can they do it?"

He told Milo what Rachel said. *That's brilliant. I'll talk to my faerie right now. He'll be able to gather people up when the timing is right. Do you have an idea of what is going to be needed to start this?* Finn told him he didn't, but he'd find some information on the Internet. *Good. Tell Rachel I love her for this.*

Finn and Rachel went into the house and to his office. Tomorrow her things were going to be delivered from her house to here. Chad was going to be using the sub levels of the house as his own until he decided what his plans were going to be. The faeries had fixed it up for him to have his own entrance too. Finn made himself a mental note to find a faerie for Chad. And soon. He should have thought of it when he first realized Chad was going to be related to him.

For the first time in ages, Finn felt as if he had a purpose. It wasn't like he didn't have a job to do, or things to fill his time. But it had felt as if he was just filling a void anyone could have filled. Today, with the help for the halfway house, his blood was stirring in a way he'd never felt about work. He was excited as he'd ever been.

The Internet proved to be very helpful after they figured out what wording to use to bring up buildings. They decided a hotel-like setting would be the best to use, simply because the rooms would be private, as well as having a bathroom for each of the rooms. After they figured out what they could build, Milo also told the group in charge what sort of amenities would be needed, as well as things not to put in each room. Such as no television—for now. Also, a cutoff switch for each separate room to make Internet connections on a day to day basis.

Milo joined them for dinner later. He, too, was excited to have something to work on. Finn was sort of sad his parents had left already. It would have been fun to share the excitement with them. After the building was built—sometime tomorrow, Lily, Milo's faerie, told them—they would take the people running the place to the new working building.

"You do know this is going to have people coming out of the woodwork for us to help them too." Milo shook his head when Finn told him good. "You don't understand. Every crackpot in the world is going to be wanting us to fund stupid projects. Like someone going to the moon, or something equally stupid."

"I hope we won't be taken by someone wanting to go there, but we'll handle it well and tell them to look elsewhere. Then if they don't take our advice, we'll take care of them with our dragons. Look at it as a win-win situation for us." Milo asked him how he came to having the dragons take care of them. "You see, they'll be out of our hair. Others will notice how the dragons took care of the crackpots and never bother us again. Also, our dragons will be happy for the fun time they have. See?"

"You're insane. You know we can't kill people just because they want to scam us." Finn jokingly asked him why not. "Because we'll have to explain why there are so many burn places in our yard to the authorities, for one."

"I'm not worried about us getting in trouble over a few scorch marks." Milo asked him why he wasn't. "Aunt Carson will have our backs."

He and Milo laughed hard about Aunt Carson having their backs. She'd be pissy about what they did, but only because she'd not been able to do it herself. Their aunt was scary when she was in a mood. Which, to him, was nearly all the time.

~~~

Sandra was going to the courtroom today to figure out her fate, she supposed. Feeling like she'd been in the ugly jail cell for years rather than a few days, she was glad to be out of doors, even if it was only for a few minutes. Inhaling deeply as they passed her from the building to the awaiting van, Sandra realized how much she missed being able to come and go as she pleased.

Having plenty of time to think, she knew her husband was being influenced by Rachel in this divorce thing, as well as locking her out of her home and the business she had claimed as her own. How she'd done it was a mystery to her, as she had told Chad several times he was to stay away from Rachel. She was a money hoarding bitch.

Putting those thoughts aside, for now, she stood up when told to as the judge entered the room. Why? Why on earth did people stand up when a man, no different than any other person she knew, came into the room? Whatever, she supposed. However he got his jollies was fine by her.

"Ms. Smart, are we going to have any trouble today?" She told him she hadn't caused any trouble at all. "I suppose you having to be taken away before things were settled wasn't anything but an everyday occurrence to you. But in my courtroom, you'll do as you're told, or I'll find you in contempt of court. I'll have you confined to the jail until your trial is over. Do I make myself clear?"

"Crystal. However, I would like to point out, I'm not being treated well at the jail. I have my own cell now, finally. But my commode is sitting out in the open without any kind of privacy. I want something done about it." He told her she was in jail and not allowed to have luxuries. "Taking a piss in privacy isn't a luxury, but a necessity. I need to have some sort of dignity given to me."

"Again, you're in jail, not a hotel. You'll live with the consequences of your actions. Now, we're going to go over the information I have here on the docket today, and you're going to keep your mouth shut. Also, and I should have told you this earlier, there will be no more cursing while in here. The vulgarity of you speaking in such a way is beneath the laws we govern with." Sandra rolled her eyes so he could see how she felt about his rule. "Do you wish to remain here or not, Ms. Smart? I'm in no mood to deal with your shenanigans today."

"Yes, I want to stay. But all these rules are making it so I can't tell you when you're wrong about something." He asked her what she was talking about. "The facts are I'm not divorced. No one came to me to sign paperwork for it, so it didn't happen. Another thing is, I'm unable to get into the restaurant I own or the house I shared with my husband, because of Rachel Merkel, or whatever her last name is."

"Her name is Rachel Manning, wife of Finn Manning." She rolled her eyes at him again. "You just sit there and keep quiet. I'd like to have your trial set up as soon as possible so you don't have to come in here and ruin my day."

"You mean if I sit here and not say anything, you'll set up my trial, so I can defend myself against these people? Do you mean I can get out of a jail cell I should never have been in in the first place?"

The judge told her it would wholly depend on the evidence and where it took them. "But you're not going to be released to roam around. I want you to be aware of everything expected of you right now. You have to have a home to go to so we can monitor your every move." She asked him if it meant someone was going to the bathroom when she had to take a piss. "Ms. Smart, the more time I spend around you, the more I realize why your husband wanted a divorce. No, there will not be any monitoring of your bathroom visits. The monitor will be there in the event you try and leave the yard of the house you're staying in. Do you understand what I'm saying to you? If there isn't a home for you to go to, you'll be required to spend time in the jail to make sure you're unable to flee the state. Also, if you curse one more time, I will charge you."

"All right. I'll be quiet. I want you to know I don't like being told to shut up. It's beyond rude for someone to tell another person to hush." She sat down and folded her arms over her chest. "Well, get going. I have things to do today, and sitting around this room while you get your heads out of your collective asses isn't getting me any closer to being free."

"One hundred dollar fine for Ms. Smart for cursing." She thought he was joking, but the man who had been talking to him all along wrote it down on a smallish notebook he took from his pocket. "Let's get this thing going, shall we?"

Her attorney stood up to try and get her the best deal, whatever the hell that was supposed to mean. When you do nothing wrong, why did there have to be deals made?

Glaring at her attorney, she wondered why on earth someone would name their kid Bartholomew Henderson. He looked like he was still in high school, but had told her he was going to do all the talking. Yesterday when he'd come to the jail to talk to her, he told her she should just plead guilty and let them fine her.

"That's the same thing as saying I did this shit. I didn't change the locks on my house. Nor did I close down the restaurant. This is just bullshit." He told her the places weren't hers at all, and it was trespassing. "Not in my own places, it's not trespassing."

"Ms. Smart, the restaurant and the house didn't have your name on them. Up until recently, the house was in your ex-husband's name." Sandra told him they weren't divorced. "Yes. You are. The restaurant belongs to your sister-in-law, Mrs. Manning."

"It's mine because I was running it." He asked her if she had an idea who was taking the money from the nightly sales if it wasn't her. "I don't understand what you're trying to say to me. I took money from the deposits. As the manager of the place, it was my right to take home an entire side of beef if I wanted to. Me taking money from the place shouldn't even have been brought up. What business is it of anyone's if I took the money?"

"Because, as I've been trying to tell you, it's not your money. Also, and you should really think on this, it's more than just the missing money. There is also a fraudulent case against you for your claims of owning something you don't. You can't go around telling people you own a place if it's not yours." Sandra had told him it should have been hers all along. "It's not, so don't bring it up again."

Here she sat, on an uncomfortable chair, trying to keep

from screaming at the people who were working hard at her having to stay in jail. This was just stupid, she thought. No one was on her side, and it was pissing her off royally.

Stewing in her own misery, Sandra tuned everything else out of her mind. There was some planning she needed to get done before she was set free from jail. Then there was the fact she'd been divorced while being locked up like some sort of criminal element. There had to be a law about how it was supposed to work.

Thinking about the first time she'd met Chad, brought on more things to be pissed off about. He'd been at a party of one of his friends. Sandra couldn't remember if it had been his birthday or someone's at the party. Either way, she'd not cared for him one bit. Sandra thought it was perhaps because he was so indifferent to the woman he was with. After finding out it was his sister, Sandra set her sights on him.

He had money, she'd heard. Asking anything about Chad Merkel, the first thing people said was that he'd been born with money coming out his ass — not anything she'd ever seen while married to him. Chad would pinch a penny until it turned back into copper just to squeeze its worth from it. Sandra smiled when she thought of her calling him names all the time.

Now she'd been told he was not only wealthy, but a millionaire to boot. This was why she was so upset with him. Withholding information about money was just plain wrong. They'd had a nice relationship with him paying all the bills and her keeping what money she made at her restaurant.

But, it hadn't been enough for her while working there. There was no way she'd have been able to eat at the very place she owned. Also, her car had been broken down more than it had been working.

Christ, she thought, the problems with having barely enough money flowing into her pocketbook had been staggering. It was the reason she'd taken to keeping out a little of the deposit each night she worked. Times when she'd been really low on spending money, Sandra would hit the restaurant about the time they were closing up and take the bank bag to the bank herself. She remembered the first time she'd just not taken the money to the bank. Sandra kept all the thousands of dollars for herself.

It had been one shopping spree after another after the first time. Sandra had been surprised Chad seemed to be oblivious to her new clothes, not to mention the beautiful diamond bracelet she'd gotten for herself. No matter what she did to have him notice something to cause a fight with him, he would just walk away.

"Bastard." Everyone in the room looked in her direction. It took her a few seconds to realize she'd spoken out loud. "Sorry. I forgot."

Paying more attention now as to what she said, Sandra thought again about Chad. He'd been a loser since she started dating him. They had gone out to nice places while dating and had a lot of fun when he wasn't upset about her spending habits. Even after he caught on she was having affairs, he'd been a decent person about it.

Where did he get off thinking he was divorcing her? Or *thinking* he could when the two of them were no different now than before? It just didn't make any sense. She had thought for about five minutes it was because he'd finally figured out there was money to be had, and he didn't want to share it. However, it didn't seem like something he'd do. Chad was anything but a deceptive person. And while she didn't like him, hadn't ever loved him, he'd been a real stand up kind of guy who any woman—well, almost any woman—would love to have. But she couldn't talk herself into loving or liking him. She didn't like his home boy ways, or his shucks and darn way of getting upset with her. She wanted passion. Anger. Maybe even a punch or two from him.

Fighting was another thing he never got right. Chad never got physical about anything. She'd hit him square in the face, and he'd just flinch and walk away. She'd seen the back of Chad more times while fighting than she had when they were in the same house. He was, she thought, a pussy.

Her attorney touching her on the shoulder, alerted her to her surroundings, pulling her from her musings about a man she shouldn't have married. Of course, she had known before the wedding that he was a sap, but today, this week, it was getting harder and harder to imagine what she'd seen in him in the first place.

Looking around to see what everyone else was doing, she didn't know what she was supposed to do, so sat there waiting. They were packing up things to leave, it looked like. It wasn't like her to tune everything out when thinking. Today, she supposed, was an off day for her. She needed to watch herself.

"What's going on?" Her attorney looked pissed off. "What the fuck is up your ass now? I didn't say anything."

"No, you didn't. Even when the judge asked you, several times when you wanted to go to trial. Couldn't you have torn yourself from whatever you were doing for a moment? Now it will be November instead of now." He laughed as he plucked lint or whatever only he could see from his jacket. "I guess you know what that means for you, don't you?"

"No. I don't. When are they going to uncuff me? I have to—"

"Yes, we all know, you have shit to do. Well, it's my pleasure to tell you that you're going to be in jail until the hearing. You're considered a flight risk, not to mention, several times over the last few days, you've been recorded telling the only other inmate at the jail how much you hate Rachel Manning, and how you were going to break her neck when you got close enough."

"They can't use a private conversation against me." The boy in a man's body just stared at her. The two guards who had brought her to the courthouse were waiting behind the man. "You are not going to be taking me back to jail. You said you'd get the best deal for me. This isn't a deal at all if you ask me. You fucked me over."

"No, Ms. Smart, you did it all on your own when you decided to embezzle money from a place you didn't own. No matter how many times you say it is yours, you're still going to be wrong every time. Mrs. Manning is pressing charges. The police station is pressing charges. Hell, it wouldn't surprise me if the entire town said you did something to them. I'd believe them too. Simply spending the last few days with you is making me second guess my lifelong dream of becoming an attorney." He stood there for a few seconds longer before speaking again. "You should use your tactics on teenagers about texting and driving. I'm betting you'd scare them straight without much in the way of threats. I'm sure they'd do it just to make you shut up. You have a good day, Ms. Smart. I'm going home to my wife and children, and won't think of you one bit."

"Wait. I'm not going back to the ugly cell. You promised me a good deal, and I don't know where you're from that you'd think this is a good deal—it's not. Now, you tell them all to come back here. I will not spend any more time in that place. I don't like it." The kid just laughed as he walked away. The two people taking her back to the jail cell approached her. "You touch me with those leggings again, and I'm not going to be responsible for how you're going to look when I'm finished."

"You can do this two different ways, Ms. Smart. You cooperate, or you don't. If you pick the first one, good for you. The second one is going to put you into a world of hurt." The big burly man laughed at her. "We come out on top either way. However, you're going to be pissing yourself all over this nice floor."

"Try it. I dare you to try anything against me." He pulled out what looked to her like a gun. "Are you going to kill me with your gun? If so, I want you to know it's going to take more than a bullet to stop me from hurting you back."

"I don't have a gun. Are you going to cooperate or not?"

She told him she wasn't going back. Like he was deaf and dumb, she thought. Suddenly every single part of her body seized up. The long wires coming from his odd looking gun were now attached to her body.

Every muscle in her body was frozen. Screaming behind her clenched teeth, tight with the Tazer, her eyes watered profusely. Urine ran down her legs in long streams. Sandra was sure she'd shit herself too. Even as they put the cuffs on her arms and legs to take her back, she couldn't breathe well, much less kill them for doing something she absolutely told them not to do.

When the pain stopped, she laid there on the floor, her body and mind a mess for what had just happened to her. Looking at the two of them giggling and laughing it up as they dragged her to the waiting van, Sandra vowed she was going to get them both if it was the last thing she ever did.

Chapter 10

Closing her eyes as Finn had asked her to do, Rachel put her hand on the top of the large stone he'd found for her. He'd gone to the faerie queen to get information on having sight. It was, she told them what Finn could do. But both of them had a stronger ability now.

"What do you feel, love? Anything yet?" Concentrating a little harder, she could hear something and told him what she was hearing. "Very well done. Perfect. Now, try and filter out the noises surrounding you, and listen to what the stone has to say. It's a living being, remember, and has stories to tell too."

It didn't seem to be speaking anything she could understand. Just as she was ready to give up and tell Finn she still hadn't gotten it, the stone spoke to her. But the laughter from it drew her into his mirth too.

I didn't know what your language would be, my lady. You are a mate to a dragon. She asked him how he'd learned that. *The dragons have been around far longer than I have been a stone of this size. Dragons, as you might know, are the magic of the world. But I could feel young Finn of the Manning Dragons close by you. What is it you wish to know?*

"I'm practicing." He told her she was doing a fine job so far. "Thank you. It's strange to think I'm speaking to a stone. I would never have thought it possible. However, I'm learning that there are a great many things people never thought was possible that do exist."

Yes, humans have been around for a very long time. I think they have gotten used to having things around them, such as me, and don't notice us as much. His laughter again made her smile. *My kind used to be used for all manner of things that we are no longer useful for. Skimming one of the smaller of us across a waterway was fun for us as well. We would hold homes up with the warmth of love seeping into us. A well too. We held the gift of water from the earth for humans and animals alike to use.*

"I'm sorry for your loss. I didn't think about what you might have felt like. Not taking advantage of your presence has hurt humans as well, I think. Also shifters. So many of them live in homes constructed by things such as man made items." She loved talking to the stone. Sitting on the ground, Rachel told him she was going to have to leave here soon. "There is this woman who is married to my brother. Or she was married to him. I think there is something wrong with her. Since I've had a chance to step back and think about her, I think she's been ill for some time."

You can seek the truth of your questions if you wish. You only need to think of her, touch something, anything belonging to her, and you will know. It might be, however, easier if you touch her. She is the source of her illness, and it will show itself better for you with a single touch. Rachel asked him if it would tell her what her thoughts were as well. *I know not this, my lady. You have a great gift of seeing things no one else will know nor understand how you can.*

"I suppose it wouldn't hurt to see if she's ill or just a mean bitch." The stone laughed, and she looked at Finn leaning against another stone apparently sound asleep. "I love Finn so much. More than I ever thought I'd love anyone."

As it should be. Of all the Mannings I have ever had the pleasure of speaking with, or even heard about from other stones such as myself, Finn's father was the best of the best. All of them are good dragons. Each of them gives back to the earth when they take something from its depths. But Xavier Manning was the kindest, most generous of all of them. Which is quite a feat, my lady, as all of them are more than any other being in the world. The stone laughed again. *This one, Finn Xavier Manning, is a man of men. A dragon too. His heart is tender yet strong. His mind is as sharp as any dagger that could be forged. He, with you at his side, will bring more goodness to the earth than anyone before or after you. I thank you for that.*

"What would be a way for me to help you and other things of the earth? I'm willing to do anything you need." He told her just speaking to him, a lowly stone, was more than enough. "I thank you for speaking to me as well. However, if you give me something I can help you with, I'd be grateful as well."

Flowers need to be plentiful. Rachel was confused for a moment, then he continued. *The faeries will need all the nectar from the flowers, you see. It will give them energy to come along, dusting us off when it gets too dirty for us to get to the sunlight. Also, you may not believe this of a faerie, but they can sometimes burrow into our hearts and be safe from storms and such. They also use the smaller versions of myself to have roofs over their heads, daggers, or spears to protect themselves. So long as dragons are here, faeries will continue to be around for every living thing in the world. It's the way it has always been. Also how it will be for all time.*

"That's the most beautiful thing anyone has ever said to me. Who would have thought rocks could be so romantic?" They both laughed. The alarm on her phone signaled it was time for them to leave for the jail. "I have to leave you. I don't want to. This has been a rare treat for me with all this other stuff going on. Thank you very much."

You are most welcome, my lady. You have an ability to speak to all manner of things now. Not just the forest, but things in your own home. Each item will tell a tale to you that you might enjoy. Not all, but a lot of them will be enjoyable.

"I'll do it. I think I'd like doing something along those lines to learn more about the things around us all the time. I think I've been missing out on a lot of things." She thought of something and decided to ask him to see if he would know. "How do I turn it off? Maybe there are some things that I don't want to know the story behind."

He laughed as he answered her. *You need only to think of the story when you touch something if you want to hear it. If you only touch something to hold onto, you will be safe, I believe. Just ask whatever you're touching to give you the story, and it will be there for you.*

As they made their way back to the house, she told Finn what she'd learned. "It was as if he was just waiting for me to come along and touch him." Finn told her it was that way with whatever they touched now. "Have you figured out what's different with your magic now? I know we were told we're both stronger."

"I was sung to sleep by the stone I was leaning against. It was the strangest feeling. It was as if it knew I was tense." Rachel asked him why he'd not told her he was tense. "Because, my love, we're due in the courthouse in a few minutes. And if I make love to you again today, we'll be late."

"Well, that settles it. I don't like Sandra even more than I didn't like her before." He cocked a brow at her. "I don't know what I was trying to say. Bear with me. I'm so nervous I think if someone were to sneak up on me, I'd die of fright."

"Then I'm glad you're immortal." They were still joking around when they got into the car with Chad in the back seat. After this meeting with Sandra, they all had a long list of things to take care of. "I don't know how long this is going to take, but the chief said he'd cut her off if she were to get too mouthy. Are you going to be all right, Chad?"

"I don't think so, but then she'll be restrained, so I don't have to worry about her getting her hands wrapped around my throat." It wasn't funny. None of them laughed because it was a good possibility that if given the chance, Sandra would kill them both. "I keep telling myself she's the bad guy in this thing. I didn't have any idea what she was doing outside our home. Hell, I didn't know what she was doing while she was in the house either. Other than, of course, bitching about how we had so little."

"My mom, she spoke to you both about what happened to your parents, didn't she?" They both nodded when Finn asked. "It was a theory for a long time, I guess, implicating Sandra in killing her parents. After a lot of research on their deaths, Mom was able to determine that it was just as the paper said— murder suicide. But she did have a hand in the deaths of your parents."

"Yes. She did." Chad turned to look out the window as he continued. "I never knew what a monster she was. Sure, we had some really loud and physical altercations when we were married. I got into the habit of walking away rather than confronting her. It was the only solution I could think of. I wasn't going to hit her, no matter how badly she beat me, both verbally and physically."

"I think it was smart of you all the way around. It wouldn't have gone over well to anyone. Especially when you factor in that Sandra has no compunction about telling lies to people around her." Chad looked at her, and she could see his hurt. "I'm so sorry you're going through this, Chad. I ache for you."

"You're going through it too, Rach. Don't underestimate your own pain. She's been hurting you in one way or the other since I married her. You did try and tell me." She didn't say anything, but she had warned him. "This meeting is the last time I'm going to make it a point to see her. I might see her out and about when she's finished with the sentence they'll have her serve — I'm not sure what will happen with the hearing. I'm looking forward to having it just done. Then we can concentrate on the better things we're doing today."

Transferring ownership of her home to Chad was the first thing Rachel was doing. He had decided, after spending the last few nights at their house, that he wanted to live there. Rachel wanted him to find himself someone to love and to love him back. Her brother deserved so much more than Sandra and the terrible things she'd done to all of them. She'd be glad to have it finished as well.

Then it was shopping for them both a car. Even with all the

money she had, Rachel had never bought herself a new car. It was something she needed, but the ones left behind when their parents were killed had been there, not being used. The same with Chad's old car.

Their parents had taught them how to save their money. Also, to use up what you had in the way of tangible items rather than tossing it aside when something newer or more advanced came out on the market. It was why she was driving a car much older than she was. Excitement raced over her when she thought of what she wanted in a new car. However, pulling up in front of the police station crushed even her good thoughts. Rachel sat there, trying to decide if she needed to confront Sandra once more.

"Are you ready?" She looked at her brother, her only friend for so long, and nodded. Then she shook her head. "Yeah, I'm right there with you. I want to be able to tell her I've gone on with my life. How it's better now she is no longer in it. Also, and I think this is what has me feeling so apprehensive about this, I don't want to hear her putting me down. Again."

"How about we have a little talk with her? If she gets out of hand or starts saying things like she normally does to us, we just get up and leave. There isn't any reason at all for us to have to put up with her abuse anymore. You're divorced, and she isn't related to either of us."

Getting out of the car, Rachel made sure Finn knew he was going with them. Rachel knew she could do it on her own, but his skin touching hers was all she needed to get through this. Chad took her other hand, and the three of them walked to the station house.

It was going to be a good visit, she told herself. Even if

Sandra was hateful to them or accused them of things they'd had nothing to do with, she and Chad were going to do this one thing, then be finished with Sandra for the rest of their lives.

"Do you remember what they told you to do?" Both her and Chad had been asked to see if they could get a confession from Sandra about their parents. Carson assured them both she was going to jail, but with the conviction for murder, it was more than likely she'd be there for the rest of her life. Finn nodded as he continued. "You don't have to do this if you're not comfortable with her answers."

"I'm not totally comfortable seeing her even knowing she'll be chained down. So we do this now, to make sure she pays for her actions, or it will haunt me for the rest of my days." Rachel told Finn she felt the same way. Then Chad spoke again. "The only thing I have bothering me is that she's been doing all this right in front of me. I never realized what she was up to. I would have — I'm not sure what I would have done, but it wouldn't have gotten this far. At least I hope I would have been able to do something about it."

"Don't blame yourself, Chad. It's over. Done." He nodded. Finn went to the front desk to tell them they were there. "We're going to walk away and never return if it gets to be too much. All right? We're not going to allow her to drag us into whatever crap she has in her mind. You and I, we've nothing to do with her ways. It's all on her. Okay?"

"Yes." Chad kissed the back of her hand he'd been holding tightly. "I don't know what I would have done without you by my side, Rach. Even when I hurt you, and I know I did, you still came through when I needed you the most."

They hugged, and when Finn came back to tell them they

were to follow the officer in charge, the three of them were put in a medium sized room with a table. There was a large eye bolt in the table, as well as on the floor. The thought of someone, including Sandra, having to be hooked up like a dog, bothered her on so many levels.

When the door opened again, a different officer asked them to have a seat, or they could just stand against the far wall. All three of them opted for the wall. Seconds later, the door opened again just after the first officer closed it, and Sandra was brought into the room with them.

To say she looked bad would have been a gross understatement. Her hair looked as if someone had taken a saw to it. It hung down on her eyes and cheeks in dirty, stringy locks. It didn't look as if she had washed it in days either.

The jumper she had on was not a color that looked good on her. It washed out her already pale face even more so. Even though it was fairly clean, she still looked a mess. As soon as she was locked to the table and floor, Chad moved to the seat directly in front of Sandra. He looked as upset as she felt for the other woman.

~~~

Finn kept an eye on both Chad and Rachel. He wasn't concerned for their wellbeing, but more their hearts. It was difficult enough for him to be here. He could only imagine what their thoughts on her appearance were. Sandra looked like she'd been in several fights, and hadn't managed to be the person on top. Moving away from the wall, Rachel joined Chad at the table.

"Hello, Sandra. You requested for us to come and see you. Here we are. What is it you wanted?" Sandra turned and looked at him first. Finn saw what he was sure the other two were seeing. Insanity. She no longer had a grip on herself. "Sandra? What did you want?"

The woman didn't acknowledge either of them sitting in front of her, but continued, for whatever reason, to stare at him. It wasn't until he shifted on his feet to try and break the tension between them that she looked at Rachel and Chad.

"You're to get me out of here. They're trying to kill me." Rachel asked her what they were doing to her. "You should know. Damn it. You've spent most of your life behind bars, haven't you? I have to get out of here before they kill me."

"No one is trying to kill you, Sandra. You're in jail. Did you kill my parents? I'd like to know the answer to whether or not you had anything to do with them both being dead." She looked at him again, then at Chad. As soon as the smile formed on her face, he knew, just knew, she'd done it. "Sandra? Did you kill my mom and dad?"

"Of course, I did." She laughed then, a maniacal laughter that sent shivers up his spine. "Had I known there wasn't going to be a big pay off to you, then I would never have married you in the first place. Damn it, Chad, why couldn't we have had all those lovely things they had? Why didn't we get to live in their big house with servants, and fucking someone waiting on me hand and foot? I would have been much happier to be with you."

"You married me for money. Is this what you're telling me?" Sandra nodded, then looked directly at Finn. Chad looked at where she was looking and turned back to Sandra. "What did he do to you? You're staring at him as if you know he's guilty of whatever is in your sick mind."

"He's a dragon. Everyone knows it. He flies all over the skies every day and kills off sheep. Did you know he's a dragon?" Chad told Sandra he did know. "I should have hired him to kill you off instead of having someone try and poison you. Think how much better off my life would have been without you there fucking it all up."

"What do you mean, you were trying to poison him? He's never done a thing to you. Neither did I. Why do you hate me so much?" Sandra explained her reasons to Rachel. "You hate me because of my looks? That's it? My looks?"

"You could do anything and get by with it because of how good you look. I was going to kill you too, but the chance never came up. I had this big plan. I was going to hold you down and pour acid all over your face so it would disfigure you. I was going to allow you to live for a year or two. Having people hide their eyes from seeing you would have been so much fun for me. But I never got the chance because you had to go and buy my big house and keep it for yourself. You should never have had a thing to do with the will. I should have had it all. Do you hear me? Every nickel should have come to me for having to endure being around the two of you all the time."

Finn nearly grabbed Rachel's back when she touched her fingers to Sandra. Whatever happened, it certainly hurt Sandra. She started screaming about being electrocuted by the bitch, as she called Rachel.

Putting her hands into her lap, Rachel started to cry. When Finn started to go to her aid, she told him she was all right. He knew she wasn't, but did stand back out of her way while she gathered her thoughts. When she looked at Sandra then, her back was ramrod straight, and her body tense with anger.

"I thought perhaps there was some sort of mental handicap you might be dealing with to make you like you are now. I hoped someone could help you so you'd be able to live a reasonably productive life. But there isn't anything wrong with you. Physically or mentally. Other than your sick ways of thinking of things to do to other people." Sandra asked her what she was talking about. "You've been like this all your life. Your parents knew there was no hope for you to change your ways when you were found killing small animals in the worst kind of ways. Even as a child, you were a monster. Not just to animals, but to other children as well. It was why they put you in the car with them when they killed themselves—to have you taken away, and their shame of having you as their child. You ruined them. They were no longer welcome at church, nor to a nice restaurant. Sandra, you really are a monster."

"They were too stupid to figure out how to make it so I could die with them. It's what they wanted. They wanted me dead. Who would want to kill me off? I was just a kid." Rachel asked her about the dead animals. "So? Every kid has a hobby. Mine was dissecting things to see how they worked. The blood was a good thing. I liked it the most."

"You killed the little boy next door to you too. Do you remember how you did it?" Sandra looked excited for a moment as if telling the reasons she might have had would have been wonderful. "Never mind—I don't care. Why did you kill our parents? I want to know why you killed them."

"Oh, grow up. How would you have been able to make it rich without them dead? You benefited from their deaths more than I did." Rachel told Sandra that she'd not been their child, so she wasn't to benefit anyway. "Yes. I got nothing from the estate because my husband was a sap in his younger years. Then the fucking prick tells me there was lots of money to go around, he just didn't want to share it with me."

"No. You have no idea how thankful I am for not sharing with you what my beloved parents left me." Chad got up, towering over Sandra. "I'm finished with you. I won't be back to hear a word from you. You're on your own. Your life is just what you wanted it to be. I couldn't care less anymore." Chad told him he'd be on the bench out front.

After he left, Sandra looked at Rachel. There were no words between either of them, though Finn knew Rachel was getting everything she needed to be able to cut Sandra out of her life as well. When Sandra's nose began to bleed, Finn put his hand on Rachel's shoulder and told her it was enough. She was raping the other woman's mind — there was little to no doubt to him of what she was doing.

Rachel stood up and turned and kissed him on the mouth. Her eyes were full of tears, but they didn't fall. Taking his arm and wrapping hers around it, they left the room without a backward glance to the woman there. Whatever she'd found out, he doubted very much she'd share it with him or Chad.

The three of them drove to the car lot in town and looked at cars. He knew what Rachel wanted in the way of vehicles; she wanted a candy apple red one with four doors. Finn was all right with her having whatever it was she wanted. Chad came to find him after they'd been there about ten minutes.

"I don't have any credit. Well, I guess I have credit, but it has Sandra's name attached to mine, and no one will lend me money. I was — I hate to ask this of you, but could I borrow money to buy me a car? Please don't tell Rach. It will only upset her more." Finn told him he'd take care of it. "Thank you. I wouldn't ask, but I'm afraid of Rach finding out and going back to the stationhouse and killing Sandra. I might not have cared before today, but she's stressed out, isn't she?"

"She is. I think we're going to go away for a little while next week. Just to clear our minds."

Chad and he went to the office of the dealership. Finn told the salesman who he was and that Chad was his newest brother-in-law. The salesman was falling all over himself trying to get the best deal for Chad. It helped to have a name people respected.

By the time Rachel and Chad had a new car each, they were all starving. Finn knew for a fact that Rachel hadn't eaten much that morning, so he was happy when she told him she was hungry too. Walking to the nearest restaurant, leaving their cars on the lot with the new ones to be cleaned up, it was nice to be able to sit down for a bit.

Finn ordered for the table while Chad and Rachel were talking about the visit. He was glad the two of them were close. It gave Rachel someone to talk to when he was working. It wasn't the only reason. The two of them needed each other because of the dealings with Sandra. By the end of the meal, the three of them were in a much better mood, as well as full. After walking back to the dealership to pick up their cars, Chad told them to take their older cars to the local high school and donate them to the shop department. The dealership was glad to do it for him.

Chad drove his car to his new home. None of them felt like shopping tonight, and Finn was happy for it. He was exhausted too. His mind and body had been so focused on today; it had interrupted his sleep last night. Thinking he'd go to bed early, he was surprised to find Rachel already in bed. She was naked and motioning for him to come to bed with her.

"Gladly." Stripping out of his clothing quickly, he joined her on the bed. When Rachel wrapped her warm body around his, his cock stretched and filled out. "You make me hard every time I look at you."

"You make me wet when I think about how wonderful I'm going to feel with you inside of me." He groaned, and she giggled. "Take me, big boy. I want to scream my lungs out."

"As you wish, my lady. As you wish."

Chapter 11

She didn't know what made her so desperate for his touch. It could have been one of a million things going on right now. Finn, with just his finger, could make her feel as if she had so much to live for. So much in life to look forward to as well.

His mouth over her breast was heavy. He didn't bite her, never made it painful, but loved her flesh like it was a part of him that he cherished. Finn would whisper little pieces of poetry to her, make her think he'd written it just for her, and no other.

"Every inch of you belongs to me. You've no idea how hard it is for me to watch as other men hug or touch you. Including my brothers." She moaned. An answer wasn't anything she could form in her mind right now. "You are the most beautiful creature ever created."

He made love to her slowly. Each time he made her come, she screamed out she couldn't take any more. Finn proved her wrong so many times more she could no longer hold her arms up to wrap around him. But he continued to love her, to mark her with his mouth.

"Finn, I need you. I want to feel you deep inside of me." He licked her pussy, having made his way down her body to the apex of her thighs. "If you take me there, I won't be able to hold back anything. The world will hear—"

It took her breath away when his tongue entered her sheath while his fingers held her open. It was a climax of all releases. Her heart stopped beating—even her blood, which she could hear pumping through her heart, stopped in mid beat. When she let the climax consume her, Rachel knew on some level she would never be the same person she was before.

Working his way up her body, Finn's cock touched her skin. It felt like a hot poker. Something so alien while making love, but it was all she could think of when he touched her. As he teased her body, Rachel came again. It was short, fulfilling, and oh so devastating to her already worn down system.

He laved his tongue over her hips, her navel, as well as her breast. Pushing her tender breasts together, he suckled at one then the other. She both wanted him to stop and to go on to do more to her.

When he entered her, filled her from toes to head, Rachel knew a special kind of love, so much of it she knew no one in the world could love as hard nor as much as she did Finn Manning. As he filled her again and again, she held on to his shoulders. Rachel gave him whatever he wanted or desired of her. She also knew he'd keep it safe, her heart and soul.

As Finn released inside of her, his body seemed to catch fire. It moved along his arms and chest until it consumed her as well. Screaming, not from the pain of it but the incredible pleasure, Rachel was sure this was the end of her. As darkness consumed her, she knew she'd be safe. Never would she be any safer than where she was at this very moment.

Waking up to a dark room, she looked at Finn as he turned on the light. "I have to take care of something. Would you like to come along or wait?"

She got up and hurried to the bathroom. "What time is it, anyway?" Finn told her it was just a little after five. "And this emergency, it couldn't wait until a decent hour?" She was laughing as she came out of the bathroom.

"No, not really. I have to go and burn something to the ground." She paused in dressing to ask him if it was something or someone. "Something. It's bad, or I'd never do this. As it is, if I don't go, there will be more deaths than there are already."

"I'm ready." She had wanted to lounge in bed all day, just for fun, but Finn seemed so serious, she was afraid not to go with him. They bypassed the front door where the cars were and headed to the back yard. "We're flying there?"

"Yes. I'm going to be going very quickly, so I want you to hold on tight." She told him she would. "When we get there, I'm not going to shift back. I'm going to take care of it in the air."

"I'm worried about you." He told her he'd be fine, then left her on the deck while he shifted. Getting on his back for this trip seemed scarier than before. Almost as soon as she told him she was ready, they were off. "Can you tell me what we're up against?"

Forest fire. A really horrific one. The fire brigade is locked in, as in there is fire all around them. Dad called me to help since we're closer. Once there, they're going to show me by lights where they need the fire to be. I'm closing the main area for the fire to burn itself out. We're hoping it works. She asked him if the rest were on the way too. *Not unless I can't do this on my own. I can, I want you to know. I've done this kind of work before.*

She could see the smoke. It was thicker than any fog or fire she'd ever seen before. As soon as she was off his back, Finn took to the skies again. Rachel turned to the fireman who was with her and asked what she could do.

"If you were a fire dragon, I could use you here." He laughed. She started to turn away but remembered she was sort of a dragon. Turning back, Rachel brought a ball of flame to her palm and showed it to the man. "Good heavens. Yes, come with me."

For the next three hours, she rode around in the back of a pick up tossing flame balls at some of the places where the fire was breaching the larger fire. It was hot, grueling work. Twice she'd changed out her clothing for something cooler, only to soak it through at the next stop.

Rachel estimated she'd been able to save about a dozen homes with her newfound power. Once, she was even able to throw a direct hit to a burning tree so several wild animals could escape. For every stop they made, more than a dozen fires were starting up.

Looking upward, she saw more dragons in the sky. Finn had called in his brothers, it looked to her, then realized it was more than likely his entire family. At the next outstation, Rachel hugged the other women and thanked them for coming to help. Rachel was glad for the extra hands, as well as the connection each of them had with one another.

When it looked like there was going to be some relief

from the fire for a while, Rachel went to find Finn. His mother had told him to rest. Rachel hadn't known about the amount of energy it took to be blowing flames all the time. When she found him, he was having his hand taped up.

"What did you do?" She knew she sounded like a harpy, but to see his dirty hand wrapped up in white gauze startled her. "Are you badly hurt?"

"No, ma'am, he's just fine. I was wrapping this up for my own peace of mind." She looked at the medic before sitting by Finn in the back of the ambulance. "You see, he's not badly burned, I promise you. And I needed to do something for someone I knew wasn't going to die as soon as they left my care."

"I'm sorry." He nodded but continued to wrap Finn's hand up. "How many lives have been lost to this? I would have thought there would have been enough time to get lots of people out."

"Some of the people, they didn't want to leave their homes. I guess they had the mindset nothing was going to bother them here today. The little animals were hurt too. A couple of vets are here helping them out. It just breaks a man's heart to know that some person did this and walked away unharmed." She asked him if they knew who this person was. "No, ma'am. We know only that it was set. By whom? Well, we'll have to work on finding him for a bit."

"I think I can help you with that." She looked at Finn when she spoke. "I want to see if I can do this. It would perhaps go a long way in making sure it's not done again around here. Okay?"

"Yes. Just be careful for me, please?"

Kissing Finn on the mouth, she made her way to the burnt out forest she'd tried to save. Walking in as far as the heat would allow her to, Rachel stopped moving when the branch of one of the larger trees stood up in front of her. It. Stood. Up. In. Front. Of. Her.

"Are you here to help, my lady? Or are you going to let us burn more?" She told the branch what her plan was. "I can help you with that, my lady. You are the mate to the great red dragon, are you not? The one that has been burning a path to save so many."

"I am. I don't know how many I was able to save from the ground. But as you know, Finn has done a great deal to ward off more burning surrounding the area." The branch told her he was a good man, as was she a wonderful woman. "I thank you for your compliment, sir tree."

"The human who has done this is now at his home. He is watching what his fire has done to so many and finding humor in it. If you were to go to the epic center of the fire—the fireman you were speaking to first can help you—you will find enough evidence to have him arrested." She asked him how he knew so very much about fire departments and such. "I've been around for a great many years. My parent tree will be able to regrow because she has been storing seeds from herself all her life. I am but one of her seedlings who didn't have enough time to put down deep roots to save myself."

"I'm so sorry to hear you're not going to live. Is there anything I can do to save you? I would hate to have you die when you've helped me so much." He told her she'd already done that by being with him as he died. "I will stay until you stop speaking to me. I'm so terribly sorry for all this."

She waited with the tree—he was actually a tree, not a branch as she'd thought. When he crumbled to the earth, another pile of cinders from the fire, Rachel hurt for the loss of him as much as she had the small animals she'd seen who hadn't been able to get to safety.

Finn was gone when she returned. The medic was working on another person. Even from where she stood, Rachel knew he wasn't going to make it. It was all she could do not to will the person to live. She also knew to wish something along those lines wouldn't mean a good life for the poor man. He was nearly gone as it was.

Riding around in the truck again, she was too exhausted to notice the animals she'd been able to free. A part of her mind was glad for it. The rest of it wanted to run away, to unsee all the things a single person had done. Remembering what the tree had told her, Rachel asked for the truck to stop for a moment.

Telling the firefighter what she knew, he was able to follow her directions to the site where the man had been camping. There was all sorts of evidence to pick up. Most of it still in good shape. But it was the hazard flames they found in a metal box that told the story. He had labeled them all for places he wanted to set the next fire and the next.

"This will help a great deal, Mrs. Manning." Rachel asked him to call her Rachel, please. "I'm not going to ask you how you found this to be here. I'm just glad we can use it against this person. And pay he will. This is a national forest. We don't take this sort of thing lightly."

"I'm sure you don't." He told her his first name was Jeff. "Thank you, Jeff. I think you and your men deserve a steak dinner after this. In fact, if you get me a list of the station houses and the people who have brought food here to feed you, my husband and I will do it just for you."

"You don't have to do anything for us, Rachel. It's our job." She told him it was a done deal as far as she was concerned, and he'd better be getting her the list. "Yes, ma'am, I will. I can't wait to tell them the famous Mannings are helping us out."

"We'd appreciate it if you didn't mention our name." Finn came out of the darkness around them and hugged her tightly. He continued when he wrapped his arms around her. "Just say a hefty donation came through, and it said to buy dinner for everyone here. I wish I had thought of it."

He kissed her again, and they spoke to Jeff as the police gathered up the evidence the fire marshall was pointing out. It made her feel good to know she'd been able to help them out, even if it meant getting someone else into trouble. By the time they were ready to call it a day, the fire was still burning, but no longer much of a threat to the homes and places of businesses around it.

~~~

Theo was working on one of the many projects he'd told Mr. Black he'd do for him. It didn't matter to him that the old buzzard had died before he'd seen the end of his requests. Theo was a man who did what was promised. He'd liked the old man a great deal.

"Theo, you don't have to do any of his list. I'm just gonna sell this old place as it is." Theo told Mrs. Black he didn't mind working on the things Harold wanted done. "Durned old fool left me here all alone. I tell you, when I get to see him on the other side, I'm going to give him a piece of my mind."

"You do that." Theo came down off the ladder and put it

down on the ground so it couldn't be used to enter the house. "Have you heard from your children or grandchildren yet? I hadn't realized you had so many."

"It's doubtful they'll take any more notice of me wanting some help than they did his funeral. Harold told me once that the kids wouldn't come to see us off on account of there being no money they can get. He was right, I guess." MaryBeth laughed. "Sure is going to mess up their day when they hear about us not only having money, but more'n they'll ever see in their lifetimes. Did I tell you my son bought himself a new head of hair? Something about plugs was his reason for not coming to the funeral. I have never heard the likes, have you?"

"No ma'am, I don't think I have. It's a shame you have to put up with something like this coming from your own children. The one you were worried about, is he going to make it?" MaryBeth corrected him. "Oh, sorry. Is she going to make it? You said her name was Pembroke, correct?"

"That's her. She's had herself a hard time of life lately. Had her locked into one of them sanatoriums or the like. I knew she'd gone into the military when she was just a kid, a grown-up kid. But all the same, I thought her too young to be going away from him." Harold had told Theo about his youngest granddaughter. She ran away to join the service to get out of the house of her parents. "Do you suppose there is ever a time when a family can come together without tearing each other up with words? I don't. Just so you know."

"My family does fine together. But then, as you know, we're not humans." Marybeth told him she wished she wasn't at times. "I think you'd make a very beautiful dragon, ma'am. Right up there alongside of my own mom. She's beautiful as a dragon."

"She should be a saint. Raising six boys all about the same age. Some of them tales you told Harold about, he'd tell them to me later. Toward the end, it was all he could talk about was you and your family." She sat down on the rocker that had been pulled into the yard so she could watch him work. "I sure am gonna miss my old buzzard. He did me wrong by leaving me here to deal with them kids of ours."

"I'll be around if you need me." She eyed him hard. "I will protect you as I would my own mother. Even though she's scary well equipped to save herself, I'd still be there if she needed me."

"I know you would be. I just know it." She looked at the ladder, then at him again. "Are you about done up there acting like a monkey with a hanging toy, young man?"

"I am. And I'm a good deal older than you are." She cackled when she laughed. "Why don't you come with me tonight to have a nice supper out? You won't have to cook, and I would certainly enjoy the company. It'll be my treat."

"You thinking of hitting on me, Theo? I'm a might smarter than them girls I see running around places half naked all the time. There be a few of them who have their sights on you to live in your big house. I don't think they'd care a fig what you are so long as you keep handing out the money and credit cards for them." He told her he was actually hitting on her. "You poop you. I swear, a woman won't know her own mind when you come to courting."

"I'm a romantic at heart. However, if a woman isn't, I can turn her into a romantic in no time. I have my ways." The two of them laughed. "You get yourself all gussied up, and I'll go change. We'll have a lovely dinner, just the two of us, and talk about your life with Harold."

"I'd like that. Nobody around wants to hear me talking about him. You do. And I know you aren't just saying it to be polite. I loved that old man." Theo told her he had loved him, as well. "All right. I'm going to go and put on the shine. Once I get myself ready, we'll hit a couple of bars before dinner. What do you say to my idea?"

"Wonderful. It's a perfect way to end the day."

When she went into the house, Theo changed. He also told his brother what he was doing so they'd keep an eye on Mrs. Black's house.

Her children? Is that who she's been telling you about? Theo told George it was them all right. *I'll be there before you leave. What do you want me to tell her when I get there? She's not figured out you're keeping an eye on things for her, has she?*

No, I don't think she has. She does, however, seem to be less tense when I'm here. They'd rob her blind if they could. The son, Patrick, has been driving by the house here a couple of times a day. I'm sure he's waiting on her to leave so he can get in. George said that was terrible. *You have no idea. Someone tried to break into her little shed last night to take her pretty Christmas ornaments. Why on earth would someone want boxes of old ornaments?*

George told him some of them were probably worth some cash. *These people sound like winners if you ask me. I'll be over there soon. Have a good night with her. I'll let you know if he comes back tonight.*

Theo was planning on it. The Black family was a family he'd come to love. He didn't want anything to happen to them if he could help it. When Pembroke came, she'd better watch herself too. Theo would have no problem making sure she understood there would be no harming her grandma, even if he had to burn her to a nice crispy slice of human ash.

Before You Go...

HELP AN AUTHOR

write a review

THANK YOU!

Share your voice and help guide other readers to these wonderful books. Even if it's only a line or two your reviews help readers discover the author's books so they can continue creating stories that you'll love. Login to your favorite retailer and leave a review. Thank you.

AWARD WINNING, BESTSELLING AUTHOR

Kathi Barton, a winner of the Pinnacle Book Achievement award as well as a best-selling author on Amazon and All Romance books, lives in Nashport, Ohio, with her husband, Paul. When not creating new worlds and romance, Kathi and her husband enjoy camping and going to auctions. She can also be seen at county fairs with her husband, who is an artist and potter.

Her muse, a cross between Jimmy Stewart and Hugh Jackman, brings her stories to life for her readers in a way that has them coming back time and again for more. Her favorite genre is paranormal romance, with a great deal of spice. You can visit Kathi online and drop her an email if you'd like. She loves hearing from her fans. aaronskiss@gmail.com.

Follow Kathi on her blog: http://kathisbartonauthor.blogspot.com/